As the gorgeous guy came up to our table, Carla squealed. "I'm going to die—I'm just going to die right now."

"Megan!" Andy yelled. "Your menu!"

I'd totally forgotten I was still holding the menu next to the candle. It had caught fire.

I screamed, dropped the burning menu, and jumped up. My chair fell over and crashed into the cart where the waiter was just lighting a flaming dessert.

Chairs went flying. People screamed. Suddenly, water shot out of the sprinklers above our table and the one next to us. I just stood there, unable to move.

The Klutz Strikes Again

Alida E. Young

For Meredith, a very special granddaughter.

Special thanks to Jeff Holland, Pam Cabak's 1986-87 fourth-grade class at Prairie Elementary School in Sacramento, California, and to the fifth- and sixth-grade students of Stone Creek Elementary School in Irvine, California.

Published by Willowisp Press
801 94th Avenue North, St. Petersburg, Florida 33702

This edition copyright © 1994 by Willowisp Press,
a division of PAGES, Inc.
Original edition © 1988 by Willowisp Press

Printed in the United States of America

2 4 6 8 10 9 7 5 3

ISBN 0-87406-697-2

One

HAVE you ever wished you could hide under a rock? Or suddenly become invisible? Or just climb into bed, cover your head with a blanket, and never see or talk to anyone ever again?

Well, I have. All my life I've been a klutz—Megan the Klutz. Oh, I thought I'd gotten over it. But now as I looked around at the super-fancy restaurant, I could feel my stomach knotting up and my hands getting cold and damp. You see, restaurants and I don't seem to get along. It's like there's an evil little elf who sits at the door of the restaurant. And when he sees me, he says to his team of evil elves, "Here comes Megan Steele. What can we do to her this time?"

Well, I was determined nothing was going to happen tonight to spoil Helen Mae's birthday party.

Chris Rhodes had invited five of us to San Angelo's newest restaurant. He'd even sent a limousine to pick us up.

We were sitting at an elegant round table in a kind of alcove. Real vines and plants twined up through a wall of copper mesh. It was like being in a jungle. The only light came from two candles on the tables and from torchlike lamps on the walls.

I was sitting nearest the aisle. Spud Walters (his parents own the San Angelo Motel) sat next to me. Next to Spud was Carla Townsend (her dad's the mayor), and beside Carla was Helen Mae Vorchek, my best friend. Chris sat next to her. The chair on the other side of me was empty—waiting for Andy Gerritson to arrive.

Spud was staring at the people at the nearest table. A waiter had pulled up a cart and was tossing a salad. "I wish Andy would hurry up," Spud said. "I'm starving."

"You're always starving," Carla told him. "I swear you could eat a whale and go back for seconds."

"Yeah, well, you're always on one of your dumb diets," Spud shot back.

"Hey," Chris said, breaking in. "This is supposed to be a party. Andy should be here soon. He said he'd only be a few minutes late."

6

The few minutes had stretched to over half an hour.

Chris caught the waiter's attention, and he came over to our table. "You wish to order now, sir?"

"No, but you might bring us an assortment of appetizers."

Chris's family is rich, and he's traveled all over—even Paris and Rome—so he doesn't seem the least bit nervous in a place like this. The five of us who grew up in San Angelo have never been any farther away from home than Los Angeles or San Diego.

Chris's ancestors founded San Angelo, but his parents just recently came back here to live. At first Carla, Helen Mae, and I all three had a crush on him, but Helen Mae's the one he likes. I'm glad she got a great-looking guy like Chris.

I thought Carla, Helen Mae, and I all looked pretty nice tonight. The three of us are about the same height, five foot six, but that's where the resemblance stops. Carla has shiny, dark hair and dark brown eyes. She looks cute in anything she wears. Helen Mae has reddish brown hair and green eyes. She looks great since she lost a little weight. Me—I'm just ordinary-looking. I have ordinary light brown hair and ordinary hazel eyes. I was glad my sister, Trish, had let me borrow her blue silk blouse. It made my eyes look almost blue.

While we nibbled on shrimp and stuffed mushrooms—I didn't try the raw oysters—Chris talked about the new raft he'd bought. The guys had been rafting before, but Helen Mae, Carla, and I had never tried it. Although Chris said it was perfectly safe, I was still nervous about going on the river the next day.

"I don't think we should take Megan on the raft," Spud said. "Things always go wrong when she's around."

"I haven't done a single klutzy thing for weeks," I said defensively.

"Oh, no? What about the other day at the mall?" Carla asked. "It's the last time I'll ever follow you up an escalator. You knocked all of us down when you fell."

"It wasn't my fault," I said. "How was I to know that woman was going to stop right at the top of the escalator?"

There hadn't been room for me to step off I fell back into Carla, and she bumped into Helen Mae, who toppled Chris back into Spud and Andy. I guess we'd looked like a bunch of dominoes knocking each other over.

"It's never your fault," Carla said sarcastically. "But somehow disaster seems to strike whenever you're around."

8

Carla can be a real pain. If I buy a sweater, she buys two. I remember when we were in kindergarten, Mom bought me a box of crayons with 36 colors. Carla had her mother buy her a set of 64.

Spud reminded me of a few other stupid things that had happened that same day at the mall, like my earring dropping into the chocolate machine in the candy store. How was I to know that Trish hadn't done a good job of setting the stone?

Sometimes I don't know why I hang around with Spud and Carla. I guess it's because we've all known each other since kindergarten. Spud and Carla are like a bad habit—and you know how hard a habit is to break.

Spud kept on about the raft. "Megan will probably punch a hole through it, and we'll all drown."

"Knock it off, Spud."

I looked up to see Andy. He smiled at me, and I felt as if I were the only person in the room. Usually when I'm near a good-looking guy I get all flustered and embarrassed, but not with Andy. He's easy to be around. He's fun and . . . special. I used to think of him as just the kid I grew up with, but lately—well, things have changed between us. As I looked up into his gray eyes, the other four people at the table faded away.

Megan, my beloved, you are the most beautiful woman in the world. I want to shower you with palaces and cars and jewels.

"Oh, barf city," Spud said.

My face felt hot as I realized I was still staring up at Andy. I don't know why I go off into these stupid fantasies. You'd think by the time you were 14, you'd get over daydreaming about a guy.

Andy took the empty seat next to me. "Spud, leave her alone. You're always picking on Megan," Andy said good-naturedly. He never raises his voice and hardly ever gets mad at people. "Haven't you ever had an accident?" he asked.

"Sure, but not like Megan does." Spud reached for a fistful of olives and bumped my elbow just as I started to bite into a large shrimp. He made me smear sauce all over my face. "See there," he said. "Any day now I expect the governor to declare her a disaster area."

"Spud Walters, you did that on purpose," I said, glaring at him.

"Never mind him," Andy said.

Andy was right. There was no point in getting mad. Spud was Spud, and he'd probably be pulling tricks when he was 80.

Andy grinned at Helen Mae. "Happy birthday. Sorry I'm late, but company came from out of town to spend the weekend with us. An old friend of Mom's"—Andy gave a big sigh—"and her kid."

"I hope they won't keep you from going to the river tomorrow," Chris said.

"They will unless I can bring the kid along. Mom says I have to bring him."

"Great," Carla said. "All we need is a sniveling little brat to spoil the day."

"Yeah, you're right about that," Andy said. He gave another long, drawn-out sigh.

I was kind of surprised by his attitude. He was always playing with the neighbor kids.

"No problem," Chris said. "It's a big raft, so it ought to be large enough for seven."

"Megan can hold him on her lap," Spud said. "Then when she falls in, we'll be rid of both of them."

Carla giggled. "Be sure to wear that blouse. The water will wash out that sauce."

"What sauce?" I looked down. A big glob of red sauce had dribbled right down the front of my blue blouse. Trish would kill me.

"Maybe you should start wearing a bib," Carla said.

I bit back a nasty remark. I refused to act like Carla.

"Can we order now?" Spud asked, taking the last shrimp and the last oyster.

Helen Mae shook her head in awe. "I don't know where you put all that food and stay so skinny. I eat one piece of pizza and put on three pounds."

"Oh, Spud has lots of empty room"—Carla said and paused—"in his head."

Spud and Carla go on this way all the time. Actually, I think they like each other. But neither one would ever admit it.

The waiter brought us huge menus.

"Oh, there are so many things on this menu. I'll never make up my mind," Helen Mae said. "Megan, what are you going to have?"

Even though she is my best friend, Helen Mae drives me crazy when she can't make up her mind.

"I don't know," I said. "It's so dark in here, I can hardly read the menu."

The people at the next table were eating prime rib. It looked good.

"Try the lobster," Chris suggested. "They fly it in fresh every day."

"I had some once, and a bunch of green and yucky stuff oozed out of it," Spud said. "Don't they have any hamburgers or pizza?"

Carla gave him a disgusted look. "Spud Walters—our resident gourmet."

12

The candle was in a glass container. I pulled it over by me so I could read the menu. I had to really get close to see the small print that described the dishes I'd never heard of before.

"Chris, have you ever tried Quenelles De Broch—"

Carla's squeal cut me off. "It's him! Look look," she whispered. "It's really him."

"Him who?" I said and turned to see an incredibly good-looking guy coming toward us. I mean, Andy's cute and has beautiful gray eyes, and Chris is very handsome. But this guy—he was totally gorgeous. Even in the dim light, you could see his deep golden tan and dark, curly hair and dark eyes.

Carla was nearly choking with excitement. "You know—he used to be the host on Video Saturday Night. And he does all those suntan commercials."

Spud muttered, "He's probably as phony as Barbie doll's Ken."

"Ssh!" Andy said. And then, incredibly, he waved at the guy. "We can ask him for his autograph."

As the gorgeous guy came up to our table, Carla squealed. "I'm going to die—I'm just going to die right now."

"Megan!" Andy yelled. "Your menu!"

I'd totally forgotten I was still holding the

menu next to the candle. It had caught fire.

I screamed, dropped the burning menu, and jumped up. My chair fell over and crashed into the cart where the waiter was just lighting a flaming dessert.

Chairs went flying. People screamed. Suddenly, water shot out of the sprinklers above our table and the one next to us. I just stood there, unable to move. In seconds I was soaked. I looked at the others. Chris and Helen Mae and Spud had managed to jump back out of the way, but Carla, Andy, the TV star, and I looked like we'd been caught in a cloudburst. My hair felt plastered to my head. Water slowly trickled down my neck and back.

Carla sputtered, Spud laughed, and Andy wanted to know if I was okay. All I wanted to do was cut my throat, slit my wrists, and bury myself alive—if somebody else didn't do it for me.

Even soaking wet, the TV guy looked good. He wiped his wet face and grinned. "Andy, is this how you welcome strangers to San Angelo?"

Andy knew him? I'm sure my mouth must have fallen open.

"Meet 'the kid,'" Andy said with a devilish grin, "Scott Zuckerman."

I plopped down on a chair and didn't even feel the water soaking into my skirt.

Two

THE Rhodes' chauffeur let me off in front of our store, Steele's Gallery and Gift Shoppe. My mother runs it now that she and Dad are divorced. Mom, my sister, Trish, and I live in an apartment behind the shop.

Hoping that nobody would see me, I sneaked in through the kitchen door. But my bad luck hadn't gone away. Trish and her boyfriend, Larry, were in the living room.

Trish took one look at me and burst out laughing. "Megan, you are the most bedraggled, pitiful, sorry-looking sight I've ever seen. What in the world happened to you?"

"I don't want to talk about it," I said, feeling as dejected as I must have looked.

Mom came out of her studio where she makes sculptures to sell in the shop. "Honey, how did you get soaked? You kids didn't go down to the river, did you?" she asked sharply.

15

"Please don't be mad at me."

"I'm not mad at you," she said. "But how did you get wet? Didn't you go to the party at the restaurant?"

"Oh, Mom, it was awful," I cried. Water from my bangs dripped down my forehead and mixed with my tears. "It was the worst night of my entire life."

Even though I was all wet, Mom put her arm around me. "Now, tell me what happened."

I told her the whole stupid story. When I got to the part where I knocked over the waiter's cart, Trish and Larry hooted with laughter.

"It's not funny! What if they make me pay for the fire damage? Why does everything bad always happen to me? What's wrong with me?"

Trish was still laughing. "Mom, are you sure a witch didn't put a curse on her when she was born?"

The witch's face is in shadow as she raises one withered hand. "A curse upon your secondborn. She will know only sorrow and misfortune. A black cloud will follow her wherever she goes. . . ."

Maybe Trish was right. Maybe I was cursed.

"You'd better get out of those wet clothes," Mom said. "Tomorrow things won't seem so bad."

I didn't really believe that. But I nodded and headed for my room. At the doorway, I stopped. "I'm sorry about your blouse, Trish. I'll pay for the cleaning."

"It's okay," she said. "I needed to get it cleaned anyway. The water won't hurt it if I get it cleaned right away."

"But what about seafood cocktail sauce?"

I got out of there fast before she started yelling.

I was getting into bed when Helen Mae phoned from the restaurant. I took the call in the hall.

"Megan?"

"It's me," I said. And before she could say anything, I blurted out, "I'm so sorry I spoiled your party."

"You didn't spoil anything—not really. I wish you'd stayed. Scott Zuckerman is just as nice as he is gorgeous. It's a super party. The manager wasn't even upset. He moved us into another room, and I had lobster and it was wonderful, and the waiter brought around a dessert cart with about a million pastries. And you know me, I couldn't decide, so I had three different kinds, and I've probably gained twenty pounds, and I just wish you were here."

"I'm glad I didn't ruin everything. Is—uh—is Andy there?"

17

"He's standing right behind me, nudging me to hurry up so he can talk to you. I'll see you at noon tomorrow in front of Yokomura's. And thanks again for my necklace. I love it."

Then Andy came on the line. "Are you okay?" he asked.

"Sure. Just embarrassed. Your friend Scott—the kid—must have thought I was a total idiot."

Andy laughed. "Actually, Scott thought the whole thing was funny. What he said was that he didn't know small towns could have so much excitement."

"Well, I'm glad he wasn't mad about getting all wet."

"Nobody's mad. Well, except Carla, and she's always mad about something. We're leaving in a few minutes. Do you want me to stop by?"

"Thanks, but I'm ready for bed. I'll see you tomorrow—that is if you still want me to go rafting. I think Spud is right. I'll probably tip the raft over."

"So? A little water never hurt anybody. See you tomorrow. And stop worrying about what happened tonight. Like I said, a little water never hurt anyone."

Andy could always make me feel better. "Thanks for calling," I said softly.

"Good night, Megan," he said just as softly. "Sleep well."

But I didn't sleep much that night. I kept having weird dreams about fires. Everywhere I walked, the earth burst into flames around my feet. Then Andy came along dressed like an astronaut in a fireproof white suit and saved me.

* * * * *

The next day, Trish waited on customers while I worked in the back room where we make jewelry to sell in the shop.

I'm klutzy when it comes to lots of things, but for some reason I'm really good at making necklaces and bracelets. I don't even have trouble with tiny little beads or delicate clasps.

Sometimes, working in the shop gets kind of boring, but I just turn on some music and daydream about doing something to make Andy and Mom and Trish proud of me— something besides being a klutz.

The military band plays "Hail To The Chief." The loudspeaker blares. Ladies and gentlemen, the President of the United States—Megan Steele. . . .

When it was time to leave, I got my beach

bag with the monogrammed *M*. I told Mom I was going and hurried out the front door.

The other kids were already climbing into Ernie Vorchek's station wagon. Ernie is Helen Mae's older brother. I squinted in the sunlight and realized I'd forgotten my sunglasses. I tore back through the shop and crashed into a pedestal that held one of Mom's sculptures. She screamed. I grabbed for the sculpture and caught it just as it toppled.

My mother came running over and grabbed the figurine she had worked on for months. She held it close, and her voice quivered with emotion. "Megan Steele, how many times have I told you not to run in the shop?"

A lot of times—would you believe at least 257? "I'm sorry, Mom. Everybody's waiting for me. And I caught it, didn't I?" I was improving, at least.

Moving more cautiously, I raced to my room. The governor could really declare my bedroom a disaster area. It usually looks like pictures of a place that's been hit by an earthquake.

I yanked out the top dresser drawer. It always sticks, but this time it practically flew out and landed on my toes. As I rummaged through the stuff that had spilled onto the floor, I smelled something sickeningly sweet.

My bottle of perfume had fallen over and was dripping into the drawer—right onto my sunglasses.

I opened the bedroom window wide to get rid of the smell. Then I rushed to the bathroom and squirted some hand soap on the sunglasses. While I was washing the glasses I noticed they weren't getting clean. I glanced at the dispenser. Oh no! I'd squirted hand lotion, not hand soap.

Forget the glasses, I told myself. This time I left by the back door, so I wouldn't get a lecture from my mother about being careful.

Our shop is on the main highway. So naturally, just because I was in a hurry, every truck, camper, and motor home in Southern California had decided to go through San Angelo on their way to the river and mountains. By the time I got across the highway, Ernie had the engine going. Out of breath, I slid into the back next to Andy and collapsed.

Andy grinned. "You look as if you've been running a marathon. We wouldn't have left without you."

Carla was sitting in the middle section "Megan is always making us late."

"Or wet," Spud said. "Have you started any fires today?"

Carla made a face. "Whew! Did you take a

21

bath in cologne?" she asked.

I ignored both of them. "Where's your friend?" I asked Andy. "Isn't he going along?"

"We're picking him up now. He didn't want to wait for me to get off work."

Andy works part time at Yokomura's Pizza Palace. It was our favorite hangout, but I wasn't sure I ever wanted to go into an eating place again.

"Why didn't you tell me you knew somebody famous?" I asked Andy.

"Mom never realized the Scott Zuckerman on TV was the son of her old friend from New York. They hadn't seen each other for years. Scott and his mom just moved out to Hollywood."

"I think he's wonderful," Carla said. "He's not a bit stuck up or anything."

As we pulled into the drive at Andy's house, we saw Mrs. Gerritson and another woman waiting outside. They came over to the car. "Scott will be out in a minute," Mrs. G said. "I'd like you all to meet an old friend from Hollywood—Kate Zuckerman. Kate, these are the girls I was telling you about."

The woman nodded to us. She was thin and bony, but beautiful like the models in the fashion magazines. She looked at us so long, I began to feel nervous. Finally, she nodded again. "I think you're right about them," she said to Mrs. G.

Carla and Helen Mae and I looked at each other. *Right about what?* I wondered.

"Girls," Mrs. G said, "why don't you drop by tomorrow about one o'clock. In fact, why don't all of you come over. We'll barbeque some ribs."

"I'll be here," Spud said.

"I guess I can make it," I said. I didn't have to work in the shop on Sundays. "But what for?"

"Yes," Carla said. "Why do you want us to come?"

"You'll find out tomorrow," Mrs. G said, and smiled mysteriously. Then she called, "Scott, are you about ready?"

Scott Zuckerman came out onto the porch as if he were making an entrance to a play. He looked younger in the sunlight than he had last night, 16 at the most. As he ambled slowly over to the car, he grinned. He had two of the cutest dimples I'd ever seen.

"Have you ever been rafting before?" Mrs. G asked him.

"You bet. I've run the rapids on the Snake, Colorado, and Rogue Rivers."

"You kids be careful," Mrs. G warned. "And be home by dark."

All of us have known how to swim since we were three years old. And everybody but Carla has taken all the Red Cross safety courses. But I guess parents never get over fussing and worrying.

Andy motioned for Scott to get in beside me, then he went around to the other side.

I hardly breathed for fear my arm might touch Scott's. Like I said, I get flustered around good-looking guys. And Scott was not only gorgeous, he was famous. I'd never been so close to a celebrity, especially one I had caused to get soaked.

"This is Megan Steele. You didn't really get a chance to meet her last night," Andy said. Then he made a big deal about putting his hand over mine so Scott would notice.

"It's nice to meet you, Megan," Scott said. Then he sniffed. "Somebody's wearing Whisper. I did a commercial for it last year." He sniffed again.

My face got hot. "It's me," I said. "I had a little accident and spilled it."

"Megan's always having 'little accidents,'" Spud said. "Like last night."

Andy glared at Spud.

Carla leaned over the seat to look at Scott. "Do you and Andy know why your mothers want to see us tomorrow?"

Andy and Scott both looked too innocent as they shook their heads. "I guess we'll all have to wait to find out," Andy said with a little smile.

I knew I could never get a secret out of him, so I changed the subject. "Scott?" I asked hesitantly, still uncomfortable talking to a celebrity. "Andy said you just moved to Hollywood. Is your dad in show business?"

"My parents are divorced," he said flatly.

As usual, I'd put my foot in my mouth. "Mine, too," I said, and shut up the rest of the way to the river.

Ernie drove right up to the edge of the water. The guys unloaded all our bags, the yellow raft, and a smaller gray raft. "Where and when should I pick you up?" Ernie wanted to know.

"There's a little beach just before you come to Jackson Bridge," Chris said. "We should get there in a couple of hours."

"But don't pick us up until about four," Andy said. "We'll probably want to swim for a while."

"Why didn't anyone tell me to wear a bathing suit?" Carla moaned.

When Ernie left, Chris passed out orange life vests.

"We're not little kids," Spud grumbled. "I

25

don't want to wear a dumb vest."

"My dad's orders," Chris told him. "We wear vests or we don't go."

Chris tossed our bags and towels and stuff into the raft. "We can put our cooler with the food and cold drinks on the little raft and tow it," he said. "Helen, you're in charge of food. Andy, you and I will paddle for the first half of the trip, then Scott and Spud can take over. Carla, you take care of the music."

I knew why Chris hadn't given me a job. They were all afraid I'd do something klutzy.

Chris waded out and held the raft steady while everybody climbed in. Nervously, I waited until last. I got seasick once on a fishing boat on the ocean. I hoped I wouldn't disgrace myself on the river. As I stepped into the raft, Spud began heckling me. "Watch out, everybody. Here comes the klutz!"

I got in without falling. We all carefully sat on the sides, but we were so crowded, I felt like a sardine in a bright yellow can.

At this time of the year, the river is smooth—at least until you pass the bridge where the rapids begin. I grabbed my bag and slathered on sunscreen. Then I pulled my baseball cap down because of the glare of sun on the water.

As we listened to music and drifted slowly

down the river, I closed my eyes against the sun.

I couldn't help thinking about why Mrs. G and Scott's mother wanted to see Carla, Helen Mae, and me. Mrs. G wasn't usually so mysterious. I didn't mind, though—it would give me a chance to see Scott again. I wanted to ask him a million questions about show business, but I was still too nervous around him.

Suddenly, a drop of water splattered against my face. I yelled and would have fallen backward off the raft if Scott hadn't grabbed me.

"What was—" I began, then saw the squirt gun in Spud's hand. "Why don't you grow up?" I said.

"Aw, you just can't take a joke."

I saw Carla glaring at me, and I realized that Scott still had his arm around me. I glanced at Andy, but he was busy paddling. "Thanks, Scott," I said. "I'm okay."

"Straddle the side," Scott told me. "You'll keep your balance easier."

"Okay. But my shoe will get all wet," I said.

He grinned and pointed to the bottom of the raft. "You'll be wet anyway. We've scraped against some submerged rocks."

In several places, water bubbled up from tiny holes.

Carla moved over closer to Scott and

perched on the side. "Is it fun to make commercials?" she asked him.

"I've been doing it since I was about two. It's okay—hard work, sometimes. I'd like to do some acting, too. Maybe get on a soap opera."

"I'd sure watch it," Carla gushed.

He talked some more about doing commercials. Carla tried her best to find out why Scott's mom wanted to see us, but he just put her off with a grin.

"When are we going to eat?" Spud broke in. "I'm starved."

"And I'm thirsty," Helen Mae said. "I'll get out the cooler."

Chris gave the paddle to Spud, then helped Helen Mae pull the small raft close. They opened the camp cooler and handed around small bags of potato chips and cans of cola. Spud grabbed two sandwiches and a hunk of chocolate cake and scarfed them right down.

While I sipped my drink, Andy looked at me closely. "You're sure turning red. I thought you put on some sunscreen."

"I did," I said. I touched my nose. It felt hot and tender. I dug the sunscreen out of my bag and looked at the tube. "This isn't sunscreen! It's only factor 4 suntan lotion!"

"It's not your bag, either," Helen Mae said. "You have mine." She pointed to the two initials *HM*. I'd only seen the *M*.

I didn't look at anybody as I got my own bag and dabbed sunscreen over my already red face, arms, and legs.

In the distance, I could see the bridge. The current seemed to be getting stronger, and I noticed that Scott and Spud were having more difficulty keeping the raft straight.

By now, my right foot was cold from the water, and the sun was burning my face. I decided that if I turned around, I could freeze the other foot and burn my back.

When I turned, I knocked the radio into the watery bottom of the raft. As I grabbed for it, I bumped into Spud's paddle. I yelled and caught hold of the paddle to steady myself. Suddenly, both the paddle and I were in the water.

I went under, and I think I must have swallowed a gallon of water. I came up coughing and choking, and all I could hear was Carla and Spud laughing. I could drown, and they'd still be knocking themselves out making fun of me. Andy and Scott started to move to my side of the raft, but Chris yelled, "Don't everybody move to that side. Spud, help Megan."

Spud gyrated his arms, mimicking the way I must have looked when I fell in. "Don't just stand there—help me," I said, and held out my arms to both Carla and Spud.

They bent over and grabbed hold of me. I jerked my arms as hard as I could. Off balance and caught by surprise, they both tumbled into the water.

When they came up choking, I grinned. "How come you're not laughing now?"

Carla looked angry enough to chew the paddle in two. "I'll get even with you for this," she sputtered.

"Cut out the games," Chris said sharply. "We're almost to the bridge."

Spud scrambled back into the raft.

Andy held out his paddle to me. "Get Carla first," I said, treading water. "I'm okay."

Andy and Scott pulled Carla into the raft. But when Andy held out the paddle for me again, I missed it. Now, the current was pulling me farther and farther away from the raft.

I heard Chris yell, "Paddle fast! We have to get her before we reach the bridge!" By then I was too busy trying to dodge rocks and boulders to hear any more.

When I bumped into a large rock, I grabbed hold and waited for Andy to paddle the raft close to me. Both Scott and Chris caught hold of me and dragged me back onto the raft.

Andy gave the paddle to Chris and knelt

in front of me. "Are you okay, Megan?"

Exhausted and choking from swallowed water, I could only nod.

"Forget her!" Carla screamed. "We're going under the bridge!"

Almost immediately we hit the churning white water.

"Hang on!" Chris yelled. "I've never done this before!"

We bumped and bounced through the rough water, and I hung on so tightly my fingers hurt. I banged heads with Andy, but I didn't loosen my grip. I thought for sure we'd crash into a boulder.

"Here, let me have the paddle," Scott said. "I've had more experience in rapids than you have."

White-faced, Chris handed over the paddle without a word. As Scott maneuvered the raft past rocks, I began to relax a little. The spray felt cool on my face. This wasn't so scary, after all. I looked at Andy, who seemed to be enjoying himself. "This isn't so bad," I yelled over the crashing of the water. "In fact, it's kind of fun."

Finally, we passed the rapids, and the quiet was almost eerie. We drifted for a bit, then Scott eased the raft close to shore. We all climbed out and sank down onto the sand. I didn't know about the others, but I was wiped out.

Chris examined the raft. "Well, it doesn't seem to have any major gashes. But we lost the small raft with the rest of the food and the one paddle."

"We'd never be able to go back upstream," Scott said. "Even if we had both paddles."

"Does anybody know where we are?" Spud asked. "I'll bet we're five miles from the bridge."

"Five miles," Carla moaned. "If you think I'm going to walk that far, you're crazy."

"Nobody's going to carry you," Spud said. "You can spend the night here. There probably aren't too many coyotes or bears."

"I'm sorry," I said. "It was all my fault."

"I told you she'd ruin everything," Spud said.

I looked over at Carla to find her glaring at me as if she were considering which method of torture to use on me.

I felt good, though. I didn't care if Carla ever spoke to me again. Maybe it wasn't very nice of me, but I was glad I'd pulled Carla and Spud into the water. For the first time since I'd known them, I'd gotten the best of them.

When Carla realized Scott was watching

her, she smiled stiffly and fluffed out her wet hair. "I must look just awful," she said.

No one contradicted her, and she got up in a huff.

We gathered up our things. The guys carried the raft. Helen Mae and I carried the bags. Carla carried a grudge.

As we pushed our way through brush and brambles to find a road, I knew that nobody was likely to ask me to go rafting again.

Three

BY the time we got home, I was so worn out that I didn't wait for Mom and Trish to come back from evening shopping. I left a note saying I was going to bed early. If I didn't leave a note, they'd think I was sick. I slept until my alarm rang at ten the next morning.

While Mom and Trish and I were eating Sunday brunch, the kitchen phone rang.

Mom answered. "Megan, it's Andy."

I licked the syrup off my fingers and walked slowly across the room. I was surprised he'd even want to speak to me.

"Don't talk long," Trish said. "I need to call Larry."

She always needs to call someone. "Hi, Andy," I said. And before he could say anything, I blurted out, "I'm really sorry about yesterday. Is everybody still mad at me?"

"Nobody's mad at you," he said. "In fact,

Chris has invited us all to come up to the mansion to swim in his pool. So bring your suit."

"But I thought your mom and Scott's mother wanted to talk to Helen Mae, Carla, and me."

"They do, but not at our house. They'll be at the mansion at one o'clock. Later on, we'll all have dinner at our place."

"Why the mansion? Come on, Andy, please tell me what's going on."

"It's a surprise," he said. "Just be ready by quarter to one. Scott's driving his mom's car."

"I'll be ready, but I'd sure like to know—for what?"

When I hung up the phone, Trish took the receiver from me. It was sticky from syrup, and she made a face. Even when she makes a weird face, she's beautiful, just like Mom. How would you like to have a mother who looks like a movie star? And a sister who's a beauty queen? It's just not fair. I'm not ugly or anything, but when I stand next to Trish or my mother, I feel like a nothing. I think somebody at the hospital goofed, and I don't really belong to this family.

Now Mom looked at me questioningly. "What was that all about?" she asked.

"Mrs. Gerritson and a friend of hers from Hollywood want to talk to Helen Mae, Carla, and me up at the Rhodes mansion. Andy won't tell me why."

At the word *Hollywood,* Trish perked up. She looked like a hunting dog who'd caught the scent of a rabbit. Trish wants to be either a dancer or an actress—maybe both. "What does this friend do in Hollywood?" she asked.

"I don't know. Her son Scott makes commercials." Trish looked even more interested. "Don't get excited," I said. "He's only 16—too young for you."

"How did you get so sunburned?" Mom asked.

I told them all about the day—including having to hike five miles back to the bridge. "The kids will probably never ask me to go anywhere again."

Trish just kept shaking her head as if she couldn't believe she had a sister who was so disaster-prone. Mom tried her best not to smile, but her lips kept quivering.

"Honey, don't let it bother you. Someday you'll look back and think it's funny."

Never. I finished my waffle in silence while Trish talked about the movie she and Larry had seen.

It was Trish's turn to do the dishes, so I went into the workroom. Whenever I'm nervous or upset I paint funny little animals and figures on rocks. It always helps me relax.

I got so involved in painting a little creature resembling a camel with a rabbit's head that I forgot about time. I looked at my watch. *Twelve-thirty!*

I put away my mess and hurried to get ready. As I raced out the back door, I yelled, "I'm going now, Mom. I won't be here for dinner. Mrs. G is barbecuing ribs."

Trish shouted after me. "But it's your turn to help with dinner."

I kept on going for fear Mom would call me back. I skidded to a stop in the drive just as Scott pulled up in his mom's Mercedes. For once, nobody could accuse me of being late.

*　　*　　*　　*　　*

When we got to the mansion, Chris told the guys to go on out to the pool. Then he took Carla, Scott, Helen Mae, and me to the theater at the north side of the huge home. A movie producer had built the Spanish-style, pink-stucco-and-tile house back in the thirties. He had used the theater mostly to show movies, but it had a stage complete with red velvet curtains and theatrical lighting. It even had an expensive sound system.

Scott looked around and whistled. "This is

great. You should see some of the crummy places where I've auditioned for commercials."

Mrs. G and Scott's mother were sitting on the apron of the stage. Ever since I was in a play this summer, I know all the theatrical terms.

"Maybe Mrs. G is casting another play," I whispered to Carla.

"If she is," Helen Mae said, "I'm leaving. I hate acting."

"If it's a play, why the secrecy?" Carla asked.

Scott grinned at us. "In my mom's business you learn to keep secrets."

"And what *is* her business?" Carla and I both asked.

Before he could answer, his mother called, "Girls, come on down front and take a seat."

More curious than ever, we sat in the front row of the theater.

Kate smiled at us. "I'm sure you're wondering why I asked to talk to you girls."

We all nodded vigorously.

"Have you heard of the Victoria Vargas Schools of Modeling and Self-improvement?" Kate asked.

"My sister went to one last year," I said.

"I've heard of them," Helen Mae added, "but I'd never be able to go to one."

Kate laughed. "I'm not trying to sell you on the school. They're conducting a nationwide search for a girl to represent them in a series of commercials. Lucy here—" she tapped Mrs. G's arm— "told me about you girls."

"But we're not beautiful and talented," I said. "You need somebody like my sister."

Carla glared at me. "Speak for yourself, Megan."

"They're looking for the girl next door—a healthy, pretty, nice girl between the ages of 13 and 15."

"I knew I should have worn more eye makeup," Carla hissed.

"Even though you three girls are all different types and coloring, you fit the basic description. But what's more important is that Lucy tells me you're all very good actresses."

"Not me," Helen Mae said quickly. "Mrs. G, you know my tongue turns to mush when I get on a stage."

"Well, give it another try," Mrs. G said. "Kate's going to have a little audition to see how you do."

Kate nodded in agreement. "You see, I'm an agent who specializes in handling young people for commercials. If any of you make it to the semi-finals of the contest, I'll sign you to a contract."

A chance to make commercials? I looked at Carla. Both of our mouths were hanging open.

"Kate has an even bigger stake in wanting to find the Vargas Girl," Mrs. G put in. "Her son Scott has already been signed to do the part of the young man in the commercials."

We all looked at Scott. *He must be really good,* I thought.

"I'm going to die right here," Carla whispered. "Imagine getting to do a commercial with him."

"I want each of you to come up here on the stage," Kate said. "Just talk for a few minutes on any subject you wish. Now, which of you wants to go first?"

We all sat like lumps.

"Okay, we'll go in reverse alphabetical order," Kate went on. "I'm always last on every list, and I hate it."

"Helen Mae, your last name starts with a V," Mrs. G said. "You get to be first."

"I really don't want to do this," Helen Mae said to me. "She only asked me so I wouldn't feel left out. Mrs. G, may I just watch?"

"That's all right," Kate said. "I never take on a client who isn't absolutely certain that this line of work is what he or she wants. You'd be surprised how many mothers drag in kids to see me. It never works unless it's the child's idea from the beginning."

"Carla, you're on," Mrs. G said. "Come on up here."

Carla gave me a look that said, *You might as well go home—she's going to choose me.*

"Don't let her get to you," Helen Mae said as we watched Carla strut to the stage. "She's not nearly as confident as she pretends to be."

The two women came down the steps and stood just below the stage. Carla practically ran up the stairs. "Where should I stand?" she asked.

"Anywhere," Kate said. "Just be natural."

Carla started talking. "Ever since I was a little girl, I've wanted to be an actress or a model or something like that. I've had ballet and singing and piano lessons and drama and speech classes. I've won prizes for creative writing. I can twirl a baton, and I'm going to try out for cheerleading this year."

"You'd think she's been doing this every day of her life," I whispered to Helen Mae.

"And if it would help to take a course at a Victoria Vargas School, I'm sure my parents would let me," Carla said so sincerely that I wanted to throw up.

"I don't know what to talk about," I said. "I haven't done half the things Carla's telling about."

Helen Mae grinned. "Neither has she. She's making up a lot of that stuff."

"That's very good, Carla," Kate told her. "I like your positive attitude."

Then Kate called me. As I slowly climbed the stairs to the stage, I started getting nervous. In the Festival Week play, I'd been a character. Now I had to get up on stage in front of a gorgeous guy and be—Megan Steele.

My hands got damp. I tripped and fell up the steps. "I'm sorry," I said. "I'm just so nervous."

"Relax. You're among friends," Kate said. "Talk about something that interests you."

My mind went absolutely blank. I mean, I couldn't think of one single thing that I was interested in. My mouth was dry. And now my sunburned nose started to itch. I glanced around the stage and saw the red velvet curtains. "I—uh—I like—red." My voice came out in a squeak. "Red roses, rubies—fire engines are red—well, some of them. Sunsets are red and there are redwoods." I knew I was babbling like an idiot, but I kept right on. "Strawberries are red. I love strawberries. Oh, but they give me hives. And then there's watermelon—of course, part of it's green. And my nose—it's red. I hate red! I'm sorry. . . ."

"That's all right, Megan," Kate said. "Please

come back and sit down."

I took a seat in the second row and wished I could disappear. Mrs. G had bragged about me, and I'd disappointed her.

"Scott, give the girls the scripts," Kate requested. "I want to tape their voices."

Scott handed us each a paper from his mother's briefcase. Kate gave us a few minutes to read over the few lines.

Carla smiled sweetly at me. "Careful you don't go up there and do something else klutzy."

"Leave her alone," Helen Mae said. "You just don't want Megan to try out, because you know she's a better actress than you."

"Oh, really? And who had the lead in the Festival Week play? Me."

"All right, Megan," Kate called. "You're first this time."

With the paper shaking in my hand, I carefully climbed the stairs. I tried to remember all the things that Mrs. G had taught me. Having lines to read was easier, and I did pretty well this time.

Kate nodded approvingly. "Very good, Megan. On the next round, I'm going to videotape you and Scott."

I came down, and Scott handed me a different script to look over. I sat in the second row next to Helen Mae to go over the lines while Carla was onstage. I watched her for a minute. She seemed tense and nervous.

I hope my voice sounds all right," Carla said. "I've had a sore throat all week."

Helen Mae leaned over and whispered, "You have her worried now. She's starting to make excuses."

"It's because she wants this so much Remember how she acted when we were both running for class president? She had the 'flu' for a week."

I made myself comfortable, propping my foot on the back of the chair in front of me.

Vaguely, I heard Carla talking onstage. "At the Victoria Vargas Schools you'll learn about makeup, hairstyling, and . . ."

I was trying to memorize the lines, and didn't notice Scott sitting down in front of me until the pain struck. My foot was caught in the crack between the seat and the back of the chair.

I yowled.

"You—you'll learn how—" Carla stammered

"Get up!" I howled. "Scott, get up!"

"You'll learn—you'll learn . . ." Carla's voice shook with anger. As she ran down the stairs in tears, she screamed, "Megan Steele, you did that on purpose!"

Four

I sat there a minute, holding my sore toes. Scott kept apologizing. "It's okay," I said, trying to smile. "Who needs toes anyway?"

Hopping on one foot, I took off after Carla. I found her out by the pool talking to Spud.

"Carla, I'm sorry," I said. "I'd never try to distract you on purpose. My foot got caught in the seat."

"Don't you even"—Carla turned toward me, then stopped abruptly and smiled sweetly— "even think about it."

"Megan, I'm really sorry about your foot," Scott said, startling me. I hadn't realized he and Helen Mae were right behind me. "Are you okay?" he asked. He knelt to look at my foot.

His concern embarrassed me. I looked around for Andy. He and Chris were in the pool with snorkels and masks and hadn't

47

seen us yet. "It's okay, Scott," I said quickly, and tried to draw my foot away.

"Take off your shoe and let me take a look at it," Scott said.

"Really—it doesn't even hurt now," I lied.

Andy and Chris saw us then. They climbed out of the water and hurried over. "What's going on?" Andy wanted to know.

"Just good old Megan again," Spud said nastily. "Disaster strikes wherever she is."

"I got my foot caught in a seat and yelled," I explained. I tried to act casual as Scott lifted my foot to examine my toes, but I lost my balance and had to grab Scott around the neck to keep from falling.

He made an exaggerated choking sound. "You may not need toes, but I need to breathe," he said with a laugh.

"I'm sorry." I'd done nothing all day except say I was sorry.

"Don't give it a thought," Scott said. "Now we're even."

"So what happened in there?" Andy asked, nodding toward the theater. "Who did Kate pick?"

I tried to explain. "We didn't finish. I—uh—when I screamed, poor Carla was so distracted that she couldn't go on with the audition."

"No, it was just an accident," Carla said,

surprising me. "I never should have let it bother me."

Spud looked even more surprised than I was. "But you said—"

Carla glared at him, and he shut up. "I was just upset for a minute," she said. "Scott, do you think your mother will let me try again?"

"Sure," he said absently. Scott raised up. "Megan, your foot looks all right, but maybe you should have it X-rayed."

Now Andy was all concern. He took my arm. "Do you want to go home?"

"Please—everybody, stop making a fuss," I said. "I'm fine. Carla, let's go back in and try again."

"Good luck, Megan," Helen Mae said, and went to change into her bathing suit.

Carla, Scott, and I returned to the theater. We found Kate and Mrs. G sitting in the front row, talking.

"Well, I wondered if you two would come back," Kate said, sounding pleased.

"Then you'll let us try again?" I asked.

"That's what we're here for. This time you'll work with Scott. Megan, you had a chance to look at the script, so you go first."

I picked up the script I'd dropped. As I climbed the steps to the stage, I tried not to limp, but my foot still hurt.

"I want you and Scott to dance," Kate said, and turned on a cassette player.

"Can you dance on that sore foot?" Scott asked.

"I'm fine. Honest," I said, determined to do better this time.

Scott and I stood in the middle of the stage. As a slow, dreamy song began, Scott put his arm around me. I looked down at Kate, waiting for her to tell us when to start, and noticed Andy there watching us.

Scott took my hand in his. Mine was so sweaty I had to wipe it on my jeans.

"Don't be nervous," he whispered. "This will be a piece of cake."

Yeah, crumb cake, I thought. I placed my left hand on his shoulder, holding the script up so I could read it. I wished I'd had time to memorize the lines.

"All right, Scott," his mother said. "Take it from the top of the second page."

I hadn't even read that far. I quickly tried to flip to the next page and hit Scott in the face. "I'm sorry."

"No problem," he said, but I thought his voice sounded a little strained. "Just try not to break up," he whispered. "Mom deliberately wrote dumb lines for us to say."

We began to move with the music. Scott

looked me directly in the eyes. In the sincerest voice I'd ever heard, he said, "I'll bet you've been to a Victoria Vargas School of Modeling and Self-improvement, haven't you?"

Girl nods, the script said. I nodded and stepped on Scott's foot.

He winced sightly, but his expression never changed. "I can tell you went to a Victoria Vargas School of Modeling and Self-improvement, because you're such a good dancer."

I nearly choked, but Scott didn't even change expression.

"Oh, yes. I've only been going to the Victoria Vargas School of Modeling and Self-improvement for a month, and I've already learned so many things."

"Such as what?" he asked, straight-faced.

"Such as hairstyling, makeup, fashion, and—" I had to turn the page, and I managed to hit Scott in the face again—"and how to burp daintily."

I started to giggle at the crazy words. Then I heard everybody laughing out front, and it was just like being in a play. I got right into the part. Very seriously, Scott and I finished the little scene.

Scott gave me a hug. "That was great. You didn't break up once."

"Thanks. It wasn't so bad. I was okay once we got going."

As I came down the stairs, Kate was nodding. "You did very well, Megan. Carla, you're next."

I sat down next to Andy to watch Carla and Scott go through the same routine. Andy didn't say anything.

"Did I do okay?" I asked.

"Sure."

I shot him a quick look. His voice had sounded flat. He was lying. He didn't think I'd done well. Disappointed, I watched Carla. She looked and sounded good. I didn't have a chance. Who wanted a klutz to represent them—especially a modeling school?

When Carla finished, Kate asked us to wait by the pool. She and Mrs. G and Scott wanted to discuss our performances.

We found Chris and Helen Mae sunning on plastic rafts. When Helen Mae saw us, she jumped off and swam over to the side of the pool. "Megan, how'd you do?"

"Oh, I was my usual self. I stepped on Scott's foot and kept sticking the script in his face." I turned to Carla. "You were great," I said generously.

"So were you," she said, with a noticeable lack of enthusiasm. "That was easy, but can you imagine talking in front of a camera and knowing millions of people are watching you?"

Millions of people? I hadn't really thought about that before. Performing in front of friends and small crowds was a whole lot different from being on TV. I wasn't at all sure I wanted any part of Victoria Vargas and her schools. Well, at least I wouldn't be disappointed when Kate told me I wasn't a good candidate for the Vargas Girl campaign.

Andy took my hand. "I know what you're thinking, Megan. TV and the stage are no different. You just talk to one person and forget the rest."

"But I thought—when you didn't say anything, I thought you thought I was awful today."

He grinned. "Stop thinking. Mom and I were both proud of you."

"Thanks, Andy, that means a lot to me. After all, you were the one who got me started in this acting stuff."

"Yeah—I did, didn't I?"

In a few minutes, Kate, Scott, and Mrs. G came out to the pool. All three were smiling broadly. Carla got a smug look on her face.

We all gathered around an umbrella table. Kate looked at Carla and me. "You're both natural and have good voices and stage presence. You both look like the girl next door, but—" She stopped. Now she was going to let us down easy.

"But," she went on, "you need to understand what entering the contest would mean. You have to be able to go to the divisional contests. That means transportation, maybe staying in hotels. You have to be chaperoned. Your parents must be willing to cooperate fully. And if by chance you make it through the first two contests and represent California, there would be a great many demands on your time. Also, as I said before, I would sign you to a contract. If you didn't win the national contest, I would hope you'd audition for other commercials."

"But which one of them did you choose?" Helen Mae asked excitedly.

"I won't keep you in suspense any longer. I'd like to sponsor both of you in the Vargas Girl contest."

Carla shrieked. "Oh, thank you, thank you. This is my dream come true."

Helen Mae hugged me. "I'm so happy for you, Megan."

I just stood there, stunned.

Kate looked at me then. "You don't seem too thrilled by the idea, Megan."

"I just can't imagine you'd want me. Everybody will tell you—something awful

54

always happens around me."

"Lots of things happened in the play last month," Andy said. "But you were great."

"Anyway, I don't think my mother could take time off work to go to the contests," I added.

"I want you both to go talk to your parents," Kate told us. "If they have any questions, they can call me at the Gerritsons'. Scott and I won't be leaving until noon tomorrow."

"Thanks, Kate," I said. "I really appreciate this. But I'm afraid I'd let you down."

"As I said, I won't encourage anyone who doesn't want to be in this business with all her heart, mind, and soul. You can let me know tomorrow."

"I don't have to wait," Carla said. "I know my mom and dad will say yes. And Daddy will take me anywhere I ask."

You could bet your life on that. Sometimes I almost feel sorry for Carla. Her dad always lets her do anything she wants, but he expects her to be the best at everything. I think if Carla entered a spitting contest, her dad would expect her to spit a mile. That's one thing about being klutzy—nobody expects too much of you.

Mrs. G drew me aside. "If you decide you want to try for it, I can drive you anyplace you need to go."

"Oh, I could never ask you to do that."

"Why not?" Mrs. G asked. "After all, I was the one who told Kate about you girls."

"Do you really think I have a chance?"

"Yes, I do," she said. "And I'd love to help you in any way I can."

"Me, too," Andy said.

I was still too bewildered by the whole idea of me—Megan the Klutz—actually trying to become the Vargas Girl. The idea was ridiculous—wasn't it?

"Ladies and gentlemen, after a long search we have finally selected the Vargas Girl. She is beautiful, talented, and as graceful as a swan. Her name is—Megan Steele. . . ."

Five

"MEGAN, don't you want to go swimming?" Andy asked.

Still in a daze, I shook my head. "If nobody minds, I think I'll go home. I want to ask my mother if I can enter the contest."

"I can drive you," Scott said. "If you need some moral support, I could talk to your mother."

I glanced at Andy's scowling face. "My foot's fine," I said quickly. "I think I'd rather walk, but thanks, anyhow. And thanks for helping me."

"No problem. If there's anything I can do—"

Carla cut him off. "Oh, Scott, I could use a ride home. I can't wait to tell Mom and Dad."

I told everyone good-bye, thanked Kate, and started to leave. "We'll see you later," Mrs. G said. "We'll eat about six."

I got as far as the gate when Andy yelled.

"Megan! Wait a minute."

He'd put on a T-shirt over his swimsuit, but still had his goggles around his neck. The goggles bounced up and down as he ran toward me. "I'll walk you home," he called to me.

As I waited for him to catch up, the sun beat down on me. My face felt as if it were burning again, and I wished I'd worn a sun hat. I was beginning to look like a scalded shrimp. "I thought you wanted to swim," I said

"I didn't get a chance to congratulate you. From what I saw, I think you have a good chance."

"There must be a million girls who'll enter the contest."

Andy shook his head. "No. According to Kate, only girls who are sponsored by somebody in the business—agents, ad agencies, Vargas modeling schools—will be eligible to enter.

"Then why wouldn't Kate use one of the girls in her own agency?"

"Because the Vargas people want a fresh new face that nobody's seen on TV before."

"I admit it would be fun, but it's just a waste of time."

"There's no harm in trying. Believe me, Kate's a pro. She wouldn't sponsor you and

Carla if she didn't think you had a chance."

"Well, maybe . . ." I said, starting to get excited at the idea.

When we got to my house, I asked if he'd come in with me. "Mom will listen to you," I told him.

"Sure, I'll come in and talk to your mom if you think it will help."

Andy followed me in through the back way. Mom and Trish were at the dining room table cutting out a dance costume for Trish.

"Mom! Trish! You'll never guess what just happened!"

"The President came through town, and you spilled chocolate syrup on him," Trish said.

I glared at her.

"You sound as if it's something good," Mom said, and smiled at Andy. "What happened up at the mansion?"

"Trish, you know that Victoria Vargas Modeling School you went to? Well, they're conducting a nationwide search for the Vargas Girl to be on their TV commercials, and Carla and I get to try for it."

Trish snickered. "You and Carla? Somebody's pulling a trick on you."

"No, it's true," Andy said. "One of my mother's friends is going to sponsor Megan and Carla in the contest."

Practically in one breath, I told them all about it. "Kate says I have to be chaperoned but Andy's mom said she'd take me to the contest if you couldn't. She even offered to coach me. And Scott—that's Kate's son—has already been chosen to be the guy in the series of commercials. Can I do it, Mom? Can I?"

When she didn't answer right away, Andy spoke up. "If you want to know more about it, come over and talk to Kate. She can explain any details."

"Wouldn't you need a bunch of new clothes—a formal gown, a bathing suit, and stuff?" Trish asked.

Andy answered for me. "It's not like a beauty contest, but Kate can tell you all about that."

Trish kept shaking her head. "I can't believe anyone would pick you, Megan. You can't go five minutes without destroying something."

"That's enough, Trish," Mom said.

"Can I try for it? Please?"

My mother nodded. "I don't see any reason why not. If Lucy Gerritson's involved, it has to be a legitimate deal."

I flung my arms around Mom's neck and hugged her. "Thanks. I promise I won't do anything dumb or klutzy."

"Famous last words," Trish muttered.

* * * * * *

The next few days, Mrs. G spent hours working with Carla and me. It was a lot different from playing a part onstage. In a play, you exaggerate the emotions. For TV, we had to learn to be natural.

On Wednesday Helen Mae called. "What are you going to wear this afternoon?"

"This afternoon?" I asked blankly.

"What are you going to wear skating?"

I'd completely forgotten. Every Wednesday during the summer, Helen Mae and I always went ice-skating. "Oh, hey, I'm sorry. I'm supposed to meet Carla up at the mansion. Mrs. G wants us to practice on the stage."

"Oh . . . well, I guess I can get Chris to go. Next week, then?"

"I'm not sure, Helen Mae. I'll have to let you know. Okay?"

"Sure. You're going to the carnival Saturday with the rest of us, aren't you?"

"I'm sorry, I can't. Scott and his mother are coming out from Hollywood to see how Carla and I are doing."

"Well, call me when you have some free time," Helen Mae said softly.

"Hey, why don't you come and watch today? I don't think Carla or Mrs. G would mind."

"That's okay. You'll do better without an audience."

"I'm really sorry, Helen Mae. I promise I won't forget next Wednesday."

* * * * *

On Saturday morning, Scott and Kate came out from Hollywood. Carla and I walked to Andy's house together. Andy had to work at Yokomura's every day, but he got Saturday afternoons off. I hoped he'd get home in time to watch Carla and me perform for Kate.

Scott, Mrs. G, and Kate were sitting on the patio at the redwood table, drinking coffee. Scott was even more good-looking than I'd remembered. Carla nudged me. "What'll you bet he'll ask me for a date?"

"Not a cent." I'd never bet against her. She always gets whatever she wants. But Scott was 16. He probably thought we were just dumb.

When we joined them, Carla managed to sit next to Scott.

"Would you girls like a cold drink?" Mrs. G asked. "Milk? A doughnut?"

"Not me," I said. I was already beginning to get nervous.

Instead of answering Mrs. G's question,

Carla asked, "Do you know when we go to the first contest?"

"One week from today," Kate answered. "You have to be in Riverside on Saturday at one o'clock."

I gulped. "So soon?"

"I won't even have time to buy a new outfit to wear," Carla said.

"You don't need anything special this time," Kate said. "Just wear something casual—jeans or a skirt and sweater. If you get past this level, then they'll tell you what clothes to bring."

"What about our hair and makeup?" I asked.

"You're both fine. Wear daytime makeup." Then Kate gave me a long look. "But it might not hurt to lighten your hair a little, Megan. Just give it some highlights."

She gave us some more advice, then pointed to a large piece of cardboard. "I want you to read what I've written on the storyboard as if you were terribly sad. Megan, you go first."

I walked over to where I could read the board easily. By now I was used to Kate's weird commercials.

"I now come before you to sit behind you, to tell you of something I know nothing about." I wanted to giggle, but I read it as if

I were about to cry. "Next Sunday, being Good Friday, we will hold a women's meeting for men only."

"All right. Now, I want you to read it with enthusiasm, as if it's the most exciting thing you've ever heard."

I did it, but not very well. "May I try again?"

"Yes, but this time I want you to look at Scott."

Scott was standing right beside the board. As I began to read, he started to suck on a lemon. My mouth puckered up, and the words came out, "I nooew com befowe yew." I stopped. "Oh, that's awful, Kate. Nobody would ever do that in a commercial, would they?"

"Probably not. But I want you girls to be able to read anything under any circumstance."

"Do you know what we'll have to do at the contest?" I asked.

"No. Instead of professionals who manage contests of this type, Vicky Vargas is handling many of the details herself. There's never been a contest quite like this one. With her, you might have to recite 'Mary Had a Little Lamb' while riding a pogo stick."

"She's a character," Scott said. "Just don't let her scare you."

Easy for him to say. He'd been in the

business since he was a little kid.

Kate worked with Carla and me for the next couple of hours—sometimes with Scott, sometimes alone.

While Carla recited a poem with her mouth full of crackers, Scott drew me aside. He put his arm around my shoulder. "Megan, when you make a mistake, just keep on going. Don't stop for anything until someone tells you." He leaned his head close to me and whispered, "Don't let on that I told you, but that might be the most important thing you have to do."

"Thanks, Scott, you've been—" I started to say "great," when I looked up and saw Andy standing in the doorway.

I quickly drew away from Scott. "Hi, Andy," I called. "Scott's been helping me."

Andy shoved the sliding glass door shut so hard I thought it would shatter.

"Andy!"

Six

"ANDY?" I called, and ran after him. I found him in the family room. He was sitting on the couch and staring at the TV, which wasn't even turned on.

"Andy, why'd you leave like that? Scott was just giving me some pointers."

"Sure."

I sat down on the arm of the couch. "Are you mad at me about something?" I asked.

"Do you really care?"

"Well, of course I do. I—"

"Megan?" Scott called from the doorway. "We're going back up to the mansion to work on the stage."

"I'll be there in a minute," I said.

"So you're not going to the carnival with the rest of us," Andy said flatly.

"I'm sorry, but Scott and his mother are only going to be here today. And the regional

67

contest is next week. I need all the help I can get."

"I noticed," he said sourly.

I frowned, trying to figure out what was bothering him. Then I remembered how Scott and I must have looked, with his arm around me and our heads together.

"Andy, after next week, maybe I won't be so busy. Anyway, I probably don't have a chance of being a finalist."

"Yeah, but what if you are? You already don't have time for your friends. And you're changing."

I knew I was changing, but I thought it was for the better. "You sound as if you're sorry I'm trying to be the Vargas Girl. You were the one who said I should go for it, you know."

"Sure, but I didn't think you'd get so involved. You're worse than Carla."

My back went rigid. "I think you're just jealous of the time I'm spending with Scott," I said coldly.

"I'm not jealous," he flared back. "I just don't think you've given any thought to the future. What if you do win and go on to make the commercial? It's one of a series. You'd have to be in Hollywood all the time."

Now I was sure he was jealous of Scott. And I kind of liked the idea. "Andy, the chances—"

68

But he cut me off. "You'd probably want to take acting lessons, and—and—what about your education?"

"Megan?" Scott called again. "We're leaving."

"Don't let me keep you," Andy said. "You'd better go with your 'friends.'"

I just looked at him for a bit. I didn't understand his attitude at all. He'd always been so supportive. "Well, I'm sorry you feel this way, Andy. But I have to go."

I hurried out to join the others. As I got into the Mercedes, I looked back at the house and saw Andy at the door. When I waved, he just turned away.

Hurt, and just a little angry, I slammed the car door. Andy had managed to spoil the whole day for me.

* * * * *

Carla and I didn't see much of the other kids during the next week. I'd had to put off Helen Mae several times. I even had to cancel the skating date with Helen Mae. Carla and I were just too busy.

I was surprised how well we got along. I was beginning to think maybe I'd misjudged her. She never once mentioned the rafting disaster or the fact that I'd ruined her tryout by yelling.

She was the one who reminded me about lightening my hair. "Paula Stevens uses Sunglow," Carla said. "She claims it works great and looks really natural. Why don't we get some tomorrow? I'll help you."

Mom wasn't very enthusiastic about the idea, but when I told her that Kate had suggested it, she said okay.

Early Friday morning Helen Mae called. "Are you getting nervous? Only one more day."

"A little. But I've been too busy to get really scared—yet. Carla's going to help me lighten my hair today. Why don't you come over?"

"I don't think so."

"Helen Mae, I'm sorry I haven't had much time to be with you lately," I said before she could hang up. "I really miss you. Come and help me do my hair."

"Are you sure it's okay—with Carla?"

"It's my hair. Please. I haven't had a chance to talk to you for days."

"Well . . . okay. What time?"

"We're going over to Lyle's Pharmacy as soon as it's open. Meet us there at nine."

Mom overheard me and said, "Not until you do some work around here. Your sister has been doing most of it recently."

"I have to go now," I told Helen Mae. "I'll see you at nine."

"I want you to vacuum the living room and dust," Mom said.

I groaned silently. I hated dusting. But I hurried to get it done and was ready when Carla stopped by.

As we headed for the pharmacy, I told her that Helen Mae was going to help us. "I hope you don't mind."

At first Carla frowned. Then she said, "I think that's great. We haven't seen much of her lately. I'll bet she's been jealous of us. I know Lisa Bowman's just dying of envy."

Lisa's the prettiest girl in our class. She probably can't stand it because we're the only two who got a chance to be the Vargas Girl.

"I don't think Helen Mae's jealous or envious," I said. I was thinking about Andy and how jealous he'd acted. I hadn't even seen him since last Saturday. I hardly listened as Carla chattered on.

We met Helen Mae at the front door. As we went up to the counter, I noticed Spud by the magazine racks looking at comic books.

"Hi, Larry. I need some Sunglow," I said. Trish's boyfriend works at Lyle's part-time.

"I think we have some left," Larry said. "Try the last aisle on the right—bottom shelf,

71

I think," he said, pointing to the row at the back of the store.

As I started to go to the last aisle, Carla said, "Oh, wait. Look at these makeup cases, Megan. I need something like this."

I stopped to look at the cases.

"I'll go get the Sunglow," Helen Mae said.

"Thanks. I'll meet you at the counter."

Carla picked up one of the cases and opened it. "It's just what we need to take to the contests. I'm going to buy this one."

"I can't afford a makeup case and the Sunglow, too." I dug out my money for the lightener and headed for the cash register.

"You were lucky," Helen Mae said and set a box on the counter. "This is the last one."

Carla and I made our purchases, and the three of us went back to my house.

*   *   *   *   *

"I've never done this before," I said. "Should I wash my hair first?"

Carla shook her head. "Do you have a spray bottle to put the stuff in? It makes it a lot easier to apply," she said in her know-it-all voice.

I found a spray bottle and handed it to Carla.

72

"Come on outside," Carla said.

We went out on the back porch. "Helen Mae, would you mind getting a bath towel to put around Megan's neck?" Carla asked.

While Helen Mae went back inside, Carla transferred the Sunglow to the spray bottle and threw the empty carton and bottle into the garbage can.

As soon as Helen Mae brought the towel, Carla started at the bottom layer of my hair. "I'm going to squirt it on your hair and work it in. But you have to be careful not to get it all over the hair that's sun-bleached."

Helen Mae came over close. "Isn't that awfully blue?" she asked.

"I've seen Paula use it a hundred times," Carla said. "It always looks kind of bluish. It'll change in 15 minutes."

When Carla finished, we went back inside to get something cold to drink. I glanced in the kitchen mirror. My hair did look dark. "Carla, are you sure this stuff is Sunglow?"

"I'm positive, but I'll get the box and check it."

She went back out on the porch and retrieved the box from the garbage. She held it out so I could read it. It was the right color.

While we waited 15 minutes, we drank diet colas and talked about the contest. That is,

73

Carla and I talked. Helen Mae didn't say much. I was beginning to think that Carla was right—Helen Mae did seem jealous of us. Wasn't she the one who had been so excited for me?

When the 15 minutes passed, I rinsed my hair in the bathroom sink. As I towel-dried it, I glanced in the mirror—and wailed, "No! Just look at me!"

"Oh, your poor hair," Carla said.

Helen Mae gasped. "I told you it looked dark."

"But the box said Sunglow," Carla said. She stood there for a moment, then rushed back out to the garbage can.

Helen Mae and I followed her. "What are you doing" I wanted to know.

"Oh, this is awful," Carla said. "The bottle says Nightglow."

"It must have been put in the wrong box," Helen Mae said.

"What am I going to do?" I moaned.

"I'd sue the company," Carla said.

"Maybe peroxide would work," Helen Mae said. "Do you have any?"

"I don't think so."

"My mother uses it to lighten her hair," Helen Mae said. "I'll go find Mom and ask her if it will take out that dark color."

I mumbled a thank-you, and slumped down on the side of the bathtub. "It wouldn't be bad if it were dark like yours," I said to Carla, "but it's a terrible color. I look as if I fell into an oily mud hole."

"Or worse. Maybe you could wear a wig."

"And have it come off like it did in the play? No thanks." I reached for the bottle and the box. "Maybe the switch didn't happen at the factory," I said.

"You think somebody switched the bottles on purpose?" Carla asked. "Somebody here?"

I nodded. "Spud was in the store. I wouldn't put it past him to do something mean like that."

"But he had no way of knowing you were going to buy it. And anyhow, it was the last box." Then she went to the door as if to see if anyone was around. "I hate to even think of such a thing," she whispered, "but Helen Mae was the one who found the Sunglow. Maybe she lied about it being the last box. She had time to switch the bottles while we were looking at the makeup cases."

"Don't be silly," I said with a laugh. "Helen Mae doesn't have a mean bone in her body. . . ."

"Well, you have to admit she had the opportunity. And I don't care what you say, she's jealous of us."

The phone rang, and I answered it in the hall.

"It's me," Helen Mae said. "My mom says you should go to a professional hairdresser. She says you could ruin your hair fooling around with peroxide and stuff."

"Thanks. I guess she's right. Are you coming back over?"

"No, I'm sorry, Megan. I have to take care of my little brother. But I'll see you tomorrow."

"Okay," I said and hung up. I turned around to find that Carla had followed me. I told her what Helen Mae's mother had said. "Helen Mae isn't coming back. She has to baby-sit."

Carla raised an eyebrow. "How convenient. She just doesn't want to face you."

"I still can't believe she'd do that to me. Anyway," I said, "I have more important things to think about—like showing my mother what happened to my hair. She's probably going to kill me."

"Good luck. I think I'll go home now. I never did like to see bloodshed," she said, trying to make a joke out of it. Then more seriously, she added, "But I'd steer clear of Helen Mae until after the contest."

I headed out to the shop to face my mother. *Was it worth it,* I wondered, losing my friends just to try to be the Vargas Girl?

Seven

THE next day all the kids met at Andy's house to wish Carla and me good luck. My mother couldn't get away from the shop. Trish had the flu, and the woman who helped in the store was out of town. Mom was almost in tears when she kissed me good-bye. "I'll be at the next contest even if I have to burn the shop down."

If there is a next one, I thought.

Carla's parents couldn't take us either. Both her mom and dad had to attend some city function.

Mrs. G offered to take us both. She said it was just as well that our parents wouldn't be there. We'd be less nervous. I think Carla was relieved not to have her dad there giving her advice and telling her not to let him down.

Helen Mae looked at my hair. "You'd never know it was that awful color yesterday."

"Mom took me to the beauty shop." Carla's words came back to me. *You have to admit she had the opportunity. And I don't care what you say, she's jealous of us.* "Luckily Mom wasn't too angry," I said stiffly.

Then everybody gathered around and wished us luck, and I forgot everything but the contest.

"If either Carla or Megan makes it through to the semi-finals in Hollywood," Mrs. G told the other kids, "you can all go along."

As we were leaving, Andy drew me aside. "I'm sorry I didn't seem too enthusiastic last Saturday." He stared at his hands. "I—uh—you're going to do just great."

"Thanks," I said softly. "That means a lot to me."

And then it was time to go.

Everybody wished us good luck. Even Spud. He gave Carla a little good-luck charm for her bracelet. "You guys can do it," he said.

As Carla and I got into the car, I thought we were lucky already—to have the kind of friends we had.

"Hey, Megan," Spud called. "Just don't do anything dumb or klutzy."

Don't do anything dumb or klutzy. I almost climbed back out of the car.

*　*　*　*　*

I always get a little carsick, and my stomach felt queasy as we pulled into the parking lot of the auditorium.

Inside, people milled around the huge room. There must have been 30 or 40 girls with their parents and sponsors, but we didn't see Scott and his mother anywhere.

Below the curtained stage, four places had been set up for the judges. Each place had a table, water, and writing materials.

Most of the girls wore jeans and shirts. A few wore party dresses and looked as if they'd just walked out of a beauty shop. Some were really beautiful. A couple of them looked as if they were 16 or 17.

The loudspeaker squawked, and a garbled voice broke into all the chattering. "Will the contestants please go to the dressing rooms behind the stage? Wait for your name to be called, then come directly to the stage, where you will be told what to do. When you've completed your turn, you may return to the audience. Thank you. And good luck to all of you."

Mrs. G hugged both of us. "I'll find Kate and Scott. We'll try to sit right down front. Just be natural and enjoy yourselves."

"She must be kidding," I said to Carla as we followed the others to the dressing room. "I feel like I'm going to throw up, and she says to enjoy myself."

"I don't know why you get so nervous," Carla said. "It's just a contest."

But I noticed that Carla kept wiping her hands on her jeans. And her voice sounded too high and a little strained.

The wait was awful. There weren't enough benches, and my feet hurt. I'd made the mistake of wearing new shoes.

We talked to two girls. Kyra Benson was sponsored by one of the Vargas schools. She was a naturally pretty blond. She had on only a touch of eye makeup, but it made her blue eyes enormous. Carla latched onto the other girl. Marianne was a tall redhead who wanted to be an actress. Carla started asking her all kinds of questions. I figured the girls who were sponsored by the Vargas schools had the best chance of winning.

Carla had said it was "just a contest." But as I stood there getting more and more nervous, I realized I really did want to win.

The two girls we'd met earlier were both called before Carla or me. Then finally the loudspeaker squawked again.

"Carla Townsend from San Angelo."

"Good luck," I said, and gave her a quick hug.

I wished I could sneak out to the wings and see how she was doing, but an attendant at the door wouldn't allow anyone out of the room.

By the time there were only three other girls besides me, I was so nervous, I had to go to the bathroom. I was in the stall when I heard my name called. I was tempted not to leave the dressing room. But I couldn't let Mrs. G and Kate down—or myself.

I hurried out to the stage to find it set up like a regular room. There was a table with food on it, a couch, easy chairs, and even baskets of flowers and treelike potted plants. I had no idea what I was supposed to do, so I just stood in the middle of the stage. I kept swallowing nervously. I remembered something Spud had said once. *Pretend everybody in the audience is in their underwear.* It helped.

Unlike a play where the audience is in darkness, the judges' stands were lighted. A gray-haired, beautiful woman stood up and came over to the stage. She wore an elegant silver-gray dress, a wide-brimmed, gray hat, and a bunch of pearls. She looked like one of those glamorous actresses on the nighttime soaps.

In a deep-throated voice with a slight accent that I couldn't quite place, she said,

"Megan Steele, I'm Victoria Vargas."

My stomach did a flip. If she was looking for a girl like herself, I was out of luck. I nodded and waited for my instructions.

"You'll notice we've placed a number of props on the set," she said. "I want you to balance something on your head and walk around while you talk for a few minutes on the subject of"—she stopped to reach for a slip of paper from a box—"camels," she finished.

Camels! I'd only seen one once in a zoo when I was seven, and it had spit at me.

"There were books on the set, but I'm afraid the other girls in their excitement took the books with them," she went on. "So make do with anything you can find. When three minutes are up, a buzzer will sound. Try to fill the three minutes. Good luck."

Three minutes to talk about camels? I did have one advantage, though. One of my favorite books as a child was one that told all about animals. And, of course, there was my hobby of painting funny animals on rocks. . . .

I hurriedly looked around the set, wondering what I could balance on my head instead of a book. I noticed a flatish round basket full of fruit. I'd seen pictures of Mexican women carrying baskets on their heads.

While I carefully balanced the basket, my mind was frantically searching for any bits of information on camels. When the basket felt secure, I very slowly moved downstage.

"There are two varieties of camels. One hump, two hump. They live mostly in the desert. They're mean, and they stink."

I'd forgotten I was supposed to move around while I talked. Very, very carefully I walked the length of the stage, attempting all the while to talk directly to the judges. I made my turns with no problem. Carla and I had practiced walking with a book on our heads. This wasn't much harder. As I talked, I gained some confidence. I even sat on the edge of the sofa and got up again with no problem. This was a cinch.

"The camel's hump contains fatty tissue. My mother says hers is on her hips."

For emphasis I slapped my own hip, and I felt the basket slip. I made a grab for it.

Too late.

The basket fell off my head. Fruit flew everywhere. One apple took off as if it had been shot from a gun. Horrified, I watched it roll to the edge of the stage, take a high bounce, and catapult right onto Victoria Vargas's table, knocking her glass of water all over her beautiful silver-gray dress.

My mouth kept opening and closing, but no words came out. I must have looked like a fish out of water.

Everybody in the place was laughing, everybody but Mrs. G, Kate, and Scott—and Victoria Vargas. I just stood there paralyzed for a moment, but then I remembered what Scott had said, *When you make a mistake, keep on going until someone tells you to stop.*

I grabbed the cloth off a small round table and put the basket with one disgusting-looking squashed banana in it back on my head. Holding the basket with my hand, I raced down the steps.

Still talking about camels, I began mopping the front of Victoria Vargas's dress. She just stood there frozen—silent.

With laughter roaring in my ears, the buzzer sounded. I adjusted the large hat, took one last wipe, and said, "Now, if I only had a camel, I'd ride off into the desert and die of embarrassment."

Then I wheeled around, and raced toward the dressing room. I flew past the two girls still waiting to go on, and headed for the rest rooms. I hid in the last stall. I never wanted to face Mrs. G, Kate, or Scott again. How could I have made such a fool of myself? Hot tears stung my eyes.

I waited there until the loudspeaker announced that all contestants could relax while the judges chose the finalists. "When we call you, return to your seats out front."

Before the last squawk of the loudspeaker had stopped, I heard girls' voices talking about the contest—and laughing about me.

"How did that girl ever get into the contest?" somebody asked.

"I was sitting near the front. You should have seen Victoria Vargas's face when that apple hit her water glass."

"And then to do a dumb thing like trying to wipe up the water."

I'll never know what possessed me to do that. I'd blown any chance I might have had.

"Hey, aren't you from the same town?" someone asked.

And then I heard Carla's voice. "Well, we're from the same town, but I hardly know her. From what I hear though, she's always doing something klutzy."

I didn't really blame Carla for not admitting we were friends, but it hurt even so.

If Carla decided to come back toward the stalls, she might recognize my new shoes, I thought. I climbed up on the toilet and bent over so no one would see me. I huddled there listening to the girls until the loudspeaker announced that all contestants should return to their seats out front.

I'd stayed bent in the weird position for so long, my neck was stiff and my right foot was asleep. I tried to shake it, and lost my balance. One foot went right into the toilet. I let out a yell of shock and disgust. Luckily no one was there to hear me.

I pulled my soggy foot out of the toilet and went out to find some paper towels. The black cloud still hovered over my head. The girls had used up all the paper towels. The only thing I could find to dry my foot was toilet paper. It stuck to my fingers and didn't dry my shoe at all.

Giving up, I went out of the dressing room. Maybe I could find a back entrance and sneak out to the car. As I passed the wings to the stage, I heard Victoria Vargas's voice.

"In most contests, they announce the runners-up first, but I'm not going to keep you all in suspense. The girl with the most points is Kyra Benson from Riverside."

I wasn't a bit surprised.

Then I heard Carla's name. She had made fourth place.

As she joined the other three finalists, Carla looked ready to burst. I was really happy for her. And maybe Mrs. G and Kate wouldn't be so upset with me.

I sighed. I'd really wanted to be a finalist. *The Victoria Vargas Schools of Modeling present the Vargas Girl—Megan Steele.*

"Megan Steele! Is Megan Steele here? Please come up on the stage."

I shook my head. I'd better stop fantasizing, my fantasies were becoming too real. I started to go look for an exit. Again, the loudspeaker blared. "Would Megan Steele's sponsor check the dressing rooms?"

I gulped. *It wasn't a fantasy. It wasn't a fantasy!*

"If Ms. Steele isn't here in five minutes, we will call the sixth-place winner to fill her spot."

In a total daze, I walked slowly out of the wings and onto the stage. With every step my shoe squished with water. As if from a distance, I heard the applause, then laughter. As I kept walking and squishing toward the front of the stage, the laughing grew louder.

Then I heard Carla. "Megan!" she hissed. "Your foot!"

I looked down. Clinging to my wet shoe was a long trail of soggy toilet paper. And then, almost as if it were someone else inside telling me to do these stupid things, I calmly pulled the paper off my shoe and hung it on the branch of the potted plant.

Eight

SCOTT and Kate came out to San Angelo to spend the rest of the weekend with the Gerritsons. That night, Andy threw us a pizza party at Yokomura's to celebrate. Our families showed up for a few minutes to congratulate us.

Carla's dad gave a speech, which was more about the mayor's race in the next election than about Carla and me. I think he just assumes that "his little girl" will always be a winner. But nothing could spoil our triumph at being two of the five finalists.

"Tell us all about it," Andy said to me, after the adults left.

"I still don't know why they picked me," I said. "Everything in the world went wrong." My face got hot at the memory of walking onstage with toilet paper dragging behind me. "It was awful."

"Talk about disasters," Carla said. "I thought Victoria Vargas was going to call out the National Guard. I was so embarrassed for you, Megan." Then she turned to the others. "You should have seen Megan trying to wipe the water off the woman's dress. I'll bet that dress cost a thousand dollars." Carla laughed and poked Scott's arm. "Don't you think so, Scott?"

It was almost sickening the way she was playing up to Scott. But so far, she hadn't won her bet. He still hadn't asked her out.

"Victoria Vargas can afford a new dress," Scott said, and smiled encouragingly at me. "I like the way you carried off the disasters with humor. I think that was the reason you're a finalist."

"Well, I'd rather get it some other way," I said ruefully. "I felt like a total jerk."

"When's the next contest?" Helen Mae asked.

Scott answered. "Next Saturday. Now that Megan and Carla have the hang of it, the next contest should be easier."

"Maybe you'll have time to go skating Wednesday, Megan," Helen Mae said. "Chris and I worked up a new routine I want you to see."

"I'm sure I can make—"

"Don't forget we need to practice walking

with something on our heads," Carla said, breaking in. Then she went back to my disaster, telling everybody how the apple fell out of my basket and catapulted into the judge's table.

"I hope I get a better subject to talk about than camels," I said.

Carla and I went on telling them all about the contest.

"And speaking of swimming—which we weren't," Andy said when we finally ran down, "we're going swimming up at Chris's tomorrow. Can you three make it?" Andy nodded toward Scott, Carla, and me.

"I'd like to," Scott said. "I haven't had a chance to work on my tan. But I think Carla, Megan, and I need to get together. I can give them some good tips."

"You mean he doesn't use a sunlamp?" Spud said in a loud whisper. "I thought all those guys in show business used makeup or went to tanning salons."

Carla gave Spud a dirty look. "I agree with Scott. I think Megan and I need to prepare for the next contest."

"How about you, Megan?" Andy asked.

"I'd love to go swimming, but I'm afraid the chlorine in the pool will affect my hair. All I need is to show up with green hair."

Andy nodded slowly. "I guess a swim cap wouldn't prevent it," he said.

"That's not really the point," Scott put in a bit abruptly. "Megan can swim anytime."

"I guess I have to agree with Scott," I said. "I need all the help I can get."

I saw the little muscle along Andy's jaw twitch, the way it does when he's upset. "Hey, everybody," I said, changing the subject. "Did you notice that I'm in a restaurant and I haven't done one klutzy thing?"

"You haven't gone home yet," Spud said.

I ignored him. "What have you guys been doing lately?" I asked. "Andy, did you get that new CD you wanted?"

But before he could answer, Carla began talking about Victoria Vargas. "You should see her. She must be in her 60's but she looks about 40. I'll bet she's had a dozen face-lifts."

"Miss Vicky—that's what she likes to be called—is pretty amazing," Scott said. "Mom says she was a movie starlet back in the forties. Then she started a line of makeup. In the sixties she opened one of the first modeling schools in Hollywood. And now she has hundreds of schools all over the country. A lot of people laugh at her. But she just laughs along with them—all the way to the bank."

I guess if Miss Vicky can handle having

people laughing at her, maybe I can too, I thought. Scott said he thought I was a finalist because I'd handled the disasters with humor. Maybe I could keep them laughing—all the way to being the Vargas Girl.

While Carla kept asking Scott questions about show business, Andy and the others sat in silence, looking bored. *I'll make it up to you guys,* I thought. *As soon as this is all over, I'll never mention the contest again. I promise.*

*   *   *   *   *

Scott and Kate worked with Carla and me all the next day. Kate gave us outrageous subjects to talk about. One was on rutabagas. Can you imagine talking for five minutes about a vegetable—especially one I'd never eaten?

The rest of the week flew by, and suddenly it was Saturday. This time, Carla's family and Mom and Trish all went along. The contest was exactly like the last one, except that I got through it with only one or two little mistakes.

Out of 25 girls, Kyra Benson came in first. Second place went to a blond sponsored by a fashion designer. I couldn't believe it when I came in third. Carla came in fifth, just points behind the fourth place winner.

I was grinning so much, I was surprised

my lips didn't crack at the corners. *Watch out world, here comes Megan Steele.*

* * * * *

Afterward, Kate suggested we celebrate at the restaurant across the street before heading back to San Angelo. "My treat," she said.

I was a bit leery of going into a fancy restaurant, but luckily I didn't knock anything over. Or spill anything on me. Or burn the place down!

When we finished eating, Kate stood up. "I want to congratulate you both," she said to Carla and me. "I'm so proud of you."

"If it hadn't been for all the hard work you and Mrs. G and Scott put in, we'd never have made it this far," I said.

"But you two applied what we taught you. I'm not even going to wait for the semi-finals next week. I'd like you both to come to my office this week and go over a contract. I think you both have great potential in television commercials."

Talk about someone floating on a cloud— that was me as we left the restaurant.

Just as we reached the sidewalk, a silver-gray limousine pulled up. A gray-uniformed chauffeur jumped out and opened the door.

Out stepped Victoria Vargas. And behind her, barking and yipping, came five large French poodles, each the exact shade of gray as Victoria Vargas's dress and silver-fox fur piece.

She spotted Scott and Kate. She nodded to Kate. "Scotty, sweetheart." She came up to him and squeezed his cheek. "How's my favorite young man?"

"Great, Miss Vicky. I guess you recognize these two." He drew Carla and me forward.

"Of course. Megan and Carla, isn't it?" she said, and graciously held out her hand.

The dogs weren't so gracious, though. As I stepped forward to shake Miss Vicky's gloved hand, the dogs yapped and lunged toward me. She handed the dog's leashes to the chauffeur. He dropped one dog's leash, and somehow I got my foot tangled in it. Suddenly, we were all wound up in barking dogs. When I tried to step backward, another of the dogs ran behind me, and I got wound up in his leash, too. I couldn't even move.

"My babies don't bite," she said, just as one of her "babies" nipped my ankle.

Scott and the chauffeur finally got the dogs and me untangled.

"Oh, I'm so sorry," I said, almost in tears.

Victoria Vargas straightened her hat and fur and smiled calmly.

"Well, my dear, you certainly know how to get my attention."

I knew right then that I'd lost any chance of becoming the Vargas Girl.

Nine

CARLA and I were eating lunch at The Diet Gourmet. She finished her skimpy salad of sprouts and greens. I'd much rather have been eating a pizza from Yokomura's, but Carla said she wasn't about to gain weight before the semi-finals next week.

I'd worked hard all morning making a necklace for Mrs. Waterbury, and I was still hungry after eating an avocado-and-alfalfa sprout sandwich.

"What are you going to wear next Saturday?" Carla asked.

"The same dress I wore to the Festival Week Ball," I said, "if it's not too short. I think I've grown an inch or so since then."

"I wanted a new dress for the semi-finals," Carla said, "but Mom said I should wait until the finals and get something really sensational."

I just shook my head in awe. Carla talked

about the finals as if she already were a finalist. "I'm probably dumb for even going to the semi-finals," I said. "After that mess-up with Victoria Vargas's poodles, I don't stand a chance."

"I'm not so sure about that. After all, you did come in third."

At the sharpness of her tone, I shot her a quick glance. Her face looked sullen.

Then she brightened and said, "Let's go over our speeches."

"Fine with me. But I have to finish Mrs. Waterbury's necklace first. It shouldn't take long."

"I just remembered something," Carla said. "My dress has a rip in it, and something's wrong with our sewing machine. Could I borrow yours?"

"Sure. And I'll let down the hemline in mine if I need to."

"While we're doing that, we can practice our speeches." Carla jumped up. "I'll get my dress and meet you at your place."

I looked at my watch. "I almost forgot. Helen Mae called this morning. She's stopping by this afternoon."

I thought Carla might object. They'd hardly spoken since the mix-up on my hair coloring. I knew Carla suspected Helen Mae. But instead, she shrugged. "That's okay," she said. "We can try our speeches out on her."

"I guess," I said doubtfully. I didn't think Helen Mae would be too thrilled about listening to Carla and me talk about the contest anymore.

"See you in half an hour or so," she said and took off, leaving me to pay the bill for both of us.

I hurried home and finished the necklace. Mrs. Waterbury was supposed to pick it up at two.

Carla showed up before I even had a chance to get my dress out of the dry cleaner's bag. "Your mom told me to come right on back to your room," Carla said. She looked around. "How do you ever find anything in here?" she asked.

Carla pushed aside some junk on the bed and spread her dress out on it. The silvery beads on the white dress sparkled in the sunlight from my window. "Try yours on first," she said. "Let's see if it's too short."

I slipped into my sky blue gown. "Zip me, will you?"

The dress fit tight at the waist, then flared out. Carla pulled up the long zipper. I looked at myself in the mirror. The color made my eyes look blue. With my new lighter blond hair, I thought I looked pretty good.

"The dress is a little short," Carla said, "but I guess it's all right."

"Well, at least I won't trip over it."

I took off the dress and left it on the bed. Then I brought Mom's portable sewing machine into my room. Carla had almost finished reinforcing the seams of her dress when Helen Mae tapped on the open door. She poked her head in and saw Carla. "Oh, I'm sorry, I didn't know you'd be working."

"Come on in, Helen Mae. Carla's just fixing her outfit for the contest."

Helen Mae hung back a little. "You're sure I won't be in the way?"

"Of course you're not in the way. Sit—" I stopped and looked around the cluttered room. "I'll get you a chair."

When I returned with a chair from Trish's room, a tense silence filled the air. I wondered if Carla and Helen Mae had been arguing.

Helen Mae held out a plate of fudge. "This is for being one of the finalists in last week's contest. I haven't congratulated you guys yet."

"Thanks." I set the dish on the dresser. "Help yourself, Carla."

"Are you kidding? And get zits before next Saturday?"

"I guess you're ri—" I began, then saw the look of disappointment on Helen Mae's face. "I guess you're just going to have to miss the best fudge anybody ever tasted." I lifted the plastic wrap and took a large piece. "Mmm," I said. "This is the best ever."

Helen Mae gave me a pleased smile. "I haven't made any since I lost ten pounds. It's too tempting."

As I was licking my sticky fingers, my mother called from the hallway. "Megan, Mrs. Waterbury is here. And there's a problem."

I made a face. "There's always a problem with Mrs. Waterbury. I might be gone for a while." I hated leaving Carla and Helen Mae alone together, but I couldn't do anything about it. Why couldn't my friends get along with each other?

"If you two get thirsty, help yourself to the sodas in the fridge."

I went out front. Mrs. Waterbury had decided she wanted a different type of clasp, so I had to change it. Then she wanted a matching bracelet. Mom told her I'd have it ready by tomorrow.

When I finally got back to my room, Carla was alone.

"Helen Mae said to tell you she'd call later." Carla held up her dress. "Thanks for letting me use your machine."

"No problem."

"You know, we never did practice our speeches. We can go over to Mrs. G's and get her to help us."

"Sorry, I have to go make a bracelet. Maybe tomorrow."

"Suit yourself, but you need a lot of work on your speech. I don't know why you chose a subject like 'How Santa Ana weather affects our behavior.' You should have taken a personal topic like I did. Why would Victoria Vargas be interested in weather?"

I shrugged. "Why would she be interested in hearing why you want to be an actress and model?"

My first choice had been about banning the use of animals to make fur coats. Then Mrs. G reminded me that Miss Vicky wore furs all the time. "It's not what we talk about that counts," I told Carla, "it's how we do it."

"Well, I'm going over to Gerritsons' even if you're not," Carla said. "Call me tomorrow."

*   *   *   *   *   *

After Carla left, I worked on the bracelet the rest of the afternoon. I helped fix dinner and did all the cleanup. Trish had done my work for the last three nights.

As I finished up and carried out a pan of scraps that wouldn't go down the disposal, my mind spun with thoughts of the future.

"Tonight, The Beautiful People *proudly present Megan Steele. We will show you her new mansion, her six limousines, and her 32-room cottage by the sea. But with all her success, she is the same modest girl she was before her meteoric rise to fame. . . .*

Somebody had stuffed the garbage can with papers. So balancing on one foot, I stuck my other foot into the can to push the papers down.

"Megan?"

I'd have jumped a foot—if I'd had another foot. I turned to see Andy coming up the walk, and lost my balance. I fell backward, pulling over the garbage can and dumping the peelings and scraps all over me.

Andy came running up. "Are you okay?"

"I think so." Only my pride was hurt. Beautiful people didn't usually lie in a pile of trash.

"I'm sorry I startled you," he said as he helped me up.

"I guess my mind was a long way off," I told him.

Andy began picking up trash. We cleaned up

the mess, and without thinking, I dropped the pan into the garbage can and started into the house still carrying the garbage-can lid.

I heard Andy snickering and realized I still had the stupid lid. I went back and retrieved the pan and slammed the lid down on the garbage can. "I thought I was all over doing these dumb things," I said disgustedly. "I just get worse."

"It's because you don't concentrate on one thing."

"I know, but I can't seem to help it. My mind feels like a revolving door spinning around at high speed."

Andy followed me into the kitchen. "Maybe you're trying to do too many things," he said.

"Yeah, or maybe somebody's trying to make me feel nervous and upset."

"What do you mean by that?"

I told him about the mix-up on the hair coloring. "Carla and I think it was Helen Mae."

"Helen Mae? You're nuts. She's your best friend."

"She *was*. But Carla and I think she's jealous of us."

"Why should she be jealous?" he asked. "She just wants you to be your old self again."

"Is that how you feel, too?" I asked.

When he didn't answer, I felt the blood rush to my face. If he didn't like the new me, that was just too bad. "I suppose you're going to tell me I should drop out of the contest. You never did want me to try for it."

"That's not true! I just thought you were letting the whole contest thing take over your life. You're getting to be as bad as Scott. All he thinks about is his 'career.'"

I was beginning to get really angry, so I snapped back at him. "Well, I'm not dropping out. So if that's why you came over, you can just save your breath."

"That's not why I came over," he said. "But I'll save my breath like you suggested. I'll see you when you come down off that cloud."

After Andy left, I realized that Helen Mae had never called back. She probably felt the same way Andy did. Well, if all my so-called friends were going to act that way, I'd find new friends. I already had two—Carla and Scott. At least they knew how I felt. They knew how much the contest meant to me.

Ten

THE next day I thought Mom was going to back out of her agreement to let me sign a contract with Kate. "Are you positive this is what you want to do?" Mom asked me.

"More than anything in the world," I told her.

When you have a mother and sister who are talented and beautiful, and you're not, sometimes you feel unimportant and useless. I guess I wanted to show everybody that I could do something.

Mom kissed me. "Go to it, then. I'll back you all the way."

"Thanks, Mom," I said, giving her a big hug. "There's Mrs. G's car now." Mrs. G was taking Carla and me into Hollywood to Kate's office since neither Carla's mom nor mine had the time.

On the way, I thought of asking Mrs. G

why Andy didn't seem to want me to win the contest. But I hated to put her on the spot.

Kate's office was on a street of businesses related to movies and television and records. Out front I noticed a TV truck from a local station near San Angelo. When we walked in, Kate's receptionist was on the phone. "Kate," she was saying, "Mrs. Wicks is on line three—again." She gave us a nod and gestured toward some chairs where several kids and their mothers were sitting.

A carnival wouldn't have been any noisier—phones ringing, mothers trying to get their kids to practice, people coming in and out.

I'd told my mother this was what I really wanted to do. But now I was having second thoughts.

Scott came out of a studio with a scared-looking girl.

"What were they doing in there?" I asked Mrs. G in a whisper.

"I imagine that's a soundproof studio where they tape voices."

When the girl and her mother left, Scott came over to us. "Hi," he said. "Mom's running a little late. Hope you don't mind waiting."

I sure didn't mind. I liked all the bustle and excitement. It took my mind off my nervousness.

108

Carla put on her helpless, poor-little-me face and looked up at Scott. "Would you have time to help me with my speech for Saturday night?"

Scott looked distracted. "I'm sorry, Carla, but I have to tape these kids' voices, and I have a three o'clock call."

A call meant he was going to try out for a commercial. That was about the extent of my knowledge of the business.

"But you'll be at the contest, won't you?" Carla asked, looking even more "poor-me" than ever.

"I wouldn't miss it. But now I have to work." He called a girl into the studio.

Mrs. G offered to go over Carla's speech with her. That tickled me, because I knew Carla had only asked Scott to help her so she could be with him.

While we waited I started talking to a boy who looked about 10. He seemed so relaxed, as if he'd come here dozens of times. "Are you one of Kate Zuckerman's clients?" I asked.

"I just signed with her, but I've been making commercials since I was five."

I couldn't remember ever seeing him on TV. I could see why he might get a lot of work, though. He looked like the typical kid—cute and freckled, with hair falling in his eyes and a great smile. "I guess you like it," I said. "Are you taking acting lessons?"

"I've been thinking about it. I don't plan to be an actor, though."

"Why not? I thought being in commercials was a stepping stone to bigger things."

"Not for me. I'm going to be a chef someday."

I started to laugh, then realized he was serious. "A chef?"

"Sure. Accomplished chefs are highly paid. When I get out of school, I'm going to France. There are good culinary schools here, but people are more impressed if you've studied in France."

I just stared at this kid. Ten years old and he knew exactly what he wanted to do with his life. "But wouldn't you miss all the excitement and glamour of show business?" I asked him.

He grinned. "It's just a job like anything else."

The receptionist called his name. "Here's the address, Jimmy." She handed him a slip of paper. "Just wear jeans and a T-shirt. Good luck."

After he left, I thought about my future. Maybe Andy was right. Maybe I had been concentrating too much on winning the contest and making commercials. But was that what

I really wanted to do the rest of my life? Even if I were good enough to make commercials, I didn't have to make a lifetime commitment. I could be an artist or a police officer—even a chef, if I wanted to. I relaxed a bit myself.

After a few minutes, Kate came out of her office and motioned for us to come in. I was surprised to find a man and a woman sitting by the desk. Kate introduced us all. "Joe Matson and Gloria Carruthers are going to tape the semi-finals on Saturday night. Because you girls live in their broadcast area, they want to do a story on you. If either of you makes it to the finals, they'll tape that, too."

Carla squealed. "I'll be on TV! I'll really be on television."

My stomach did a dive like an elevator with a broken cable. "You mean everybody in San Angelo will see us Saturday night?"

The woman laughed. "Well, let's hope a lot of them do." She turned to Kate. "Where can we interview the girls?"

"Use this room," Kate said. "I have some other things to do. When you girls are finished, we'll talk through the contracts and go over any questions you might have. You'll need to take the contracts home for your parents to sign, but I want you girls to understand the provisions, too."

Joe set up a video camera and filmed us while Gloria asked questions. I let Carla do most of the talking about why we'd entered the contest and what it would mean to us to win.

"It would be the biggest thing that ever happened in my life," Carla said.

"And how about you, Megan?" Gloria asked, putting the mike up to my face.

"I think it would open a whole new world for me—a scary one. But I don't even want to think about that. I have to get past this next contest first."

Gloria gave me a consoling smile as if she felt sorry for me. "We saw the regionals. You do seem to be a bit accident-prone."

Carla giggled. "That's why they call her Megan the Klutz."

I tried not to show any expression, but I could have strangled Carla. "Well," I said, "I guess if a klutzy person can win a contest, then *anybody* can."

* * * * * *

I hadn't seen Andy or Helen Mae all week. Helen Mae never did call me, so I phoned her on Friday night. I never mentioned that she had said she'd call me. I thanked her again for the fudge. "I think it was the best you've ever made," I told her.

"Thanks." Her voice sounded a little cool.

"Are you going to the semi-finals tomorrow night?" I asked in an offhand tone.

She paused for a long moment. "I—uh— I'm not sure."

Well, I sure wasn't about to beg her. If she didn't want to come and watch the most important thing in my life, she was no friend of mine. "I have to go," I said quickly. "I have a million things to do."

I hung up before she could say anything else. I was plenty hurt, though. I almost called her back, but I didn't know what to say. This should have been a happy time. Instead, I felt depressed. I'd lost a friend, and there was a big empty spot inside me.

Saturday morning I awakened to the sound of wind. Even at seven the air felt hot and dry. A layer of oily, black dust covered the windowsill and my dresser top.

At breakfast, I snapped at Trish because she'd forgotten to finish a necklace she'd promised to do for me. "Don't worry," she snapped right back. "I said I'd do it, and I will!"

I had my hair done at the beauty salon. It looked great until I had to go outside. The hot, gusty wind practically blew all the curl out.

I nearly went crazy until we were ready to leave. Mom closed up the shop early to allow extra time for any problems on the drive to Hollywood. Trish's boyfriend, Larry, had offered to take Mom and Trish and me. Carla and Spud were going to ride with us, too. Carla's parents were bringing a whole carload of people. At the last minute, my mother decided to go with the Gerritsons. She can't stand the kind of music Larry plays in his car.

I wore old jeans and a blouse that buttoned I didn't want to ruin my hair any more than it already was. When I got in Larry's car I hung my gown on a hook so it wouldn't get wrinkled Trish had promised to do my makeup when we got there. I might not be beautiful like my sister, but I'd look as good as possible.

Spud was at Carla's house, so we picked them both up there. Carla started complaining the minute she climbed into the backseat. "Megan Steele, you brought on these lousy Santa Ana winds."

"Me? Why me?"

"I told you not to give a speech on Santa Ana weather. Now, you've jinxed us."

Spud gave his whinny of a laugh. "Can you imagine what the weather would be like if Megan was a klutzy Mother Nature? It boggles the mind," he said sarcastically.

"Hey, Spud," Larry said, "I haven't seen you in Lyle's reading all the comic books lately."

"I've been pretty busy," Spud said, looking a bit embarrassed because he never bought the books.

"I thought by now your hair would be a lot darker," Larry said.

"Megan," Carla said, breaking in, "where's Andy? I thought he'd be coming with us."

"I don't know," I told her, "I haven't seen him for several days."

"He thought he might have to work tonight," Spud said.

"It's no big deal," I told them. But it was. He could have found someone to take his place if he'd wanted to. "Larry, don't you have air-conditioning?" I asked crossly. "It's stifling in here, and it's too windy to open the windows."

"I do, but it's not working right now."

I almost always get carsick, and I was already feeling crummy. The hot air just made it worse. By the time we arrived, the auditorium was already crowded and noisy. Kate and Scott met us by the door, or we never would have found them. A bunch of girls surrounded Scott, asking him questions and getting his autograph.

"Someday people will ask me for my autograph," Carla whispered to me.

"I received a letter on the contest rules," Kate said. "It's different from the first two contests. The contestants have to stay in the dressing rooms before and after they perform. And only the sponsors can be with them."

"But Trish has to do my hair and makeup," I said.

"Sorry. You're stuck with me."

Scott finally got away from his fans. "Who else is coming?" he wanted to know. "I've saved a block of seats in the second row, but I can't hold them for long."

"Mom and the Gerritsons should be here," I said, beginning to worry about them. "They started out about the same time we did."

"They're probably having trouble finding a parking space," Scott said.

Kate nodded. "I had no idea so many people were coming. I think Miss Vicky must have invited everyone in town."

That didn't help my nerves any.

"We'd better get backstage," Kate said.

"Where's the makeup kit?" I asked, beginning to panic. "Did anybody bring in my dress?" I felt so nervous now that I couldn't have remembered my own name.

"Here's the dress and kit," Trish said. She

gave me a hug. "Calm down. You're going to be fine. Just be sure to put on some blusher. You look awfully pale."

"Yeah, Meg," Spud said. "You didn't tell us you were trying out for Miss Zombie."

Scott gave both Carla and me a kiss on the cheek for luck. I thought Carla was going to faint right on the spot.

Kate hurried us backstage. Fifteen girls from the Western region were getting ready. They were all really pretty, and they all looked more sophisticated than Carla and I did.

Kyra looked especially good in a pink dress that made her face look rosy. She didn't wear as much makeup as the other girls, and she wasn't as beautiful. But I still thought she had the best chance of winning. In fact, I didn't see how Carla or I either one had a chance against any of the contestants.

With everyone talking at once, the noise level backstage was almost as high as it had been in the auditorium. A girl from Oregon was complaining about the hot, dry wind. One from Los Angeles told her she was lucky it wasn't smoggy.

I felt hot and sticky and still a bit nauseated. I'd have given anything for a cool shower. Carla put on her dress, but I waited. I didn't want to sweat all over it.

While Carla and I stood in line to use one of the six benches in front of a mirror, Miss Vicky came in. She was wearing a different silver-gray dress, and even in the hot weather, she had on a fur.

Miss Vicky talked casually with us for a few minutes, trying to put us at ease. "Any questions?" she asked.

"Are the girls going out alphabetically?" one of the sponsors wanted to know.

"No, they'll draw numbers from my hat." Miss Vicky smiled to show perfect teeth. She took off her big, floppy-brimmed hat and dropped in a handful of numbers.

Carla picked 7. "That's my lucky number," she whispered.

I drew number 12, which meant I had a long wait before I'd be called.

"Now, remember, girls," Miss Vicky said. "Come out to the stage when your number is announced. Then I'll tell you what to do. As soon as you're through, return here until you're all called back to the stage to hear the results. You're lovely girls, and I wish you all could win. Thank you for your participation." She blew us a little kiss. "Good luck, everybody."

After she left, the room was silent for a minute, then everyone began talking at once.

Kate helped me with my makeup and hair, then I got out of my jeans and shirt. I unzipped the gown and stepped into it. But when I tried to pull it up it felt too tight.

"I can't have gained weight," I moaned.

"It's probably because you're sweaty and sticky," Carla said. "Mine was kind of hard to get on, too. Here, let me help you."

The more I struggled, the sweatier I got. Finally, I managed to get it on.

"Now, suck it in, so I can zip it," Carla told me.

"I'm never going to be able to breathe," I said as Carla slowly inched the zipper up.

"You must have eaten too much of Helen Mae's fudge." Carla laughed. "You don't suppose she had that in mind?"

"It wasn't the fudge. Maybe this weather caused me to get all puffy or something."

"Are you going to be all right?" Kate asked.

"I guess so—if I don't have to take a deep breath!"

"Now you know what women used to go through when they wore corsets," Kate said. "Why don't both of you find a place where you can sit down and try to relax?"

"I think I'll stand," I said. "I'm afraid I'll pop something." Tomorrow, I'd definitely have to go on a diet.

I found a corner by myself and leaned against the wall. Part of me wanted to be a finalist more than anything in the world. Another part of me remembered the looks on Andy's and Helen Mae's faces. Was Andy right? Had I changed—for the worse?

The judge enters the courtroom. "This court is now in session. Judge Andrew Gerritson presiding. Will the defendant please rise and face the jury?"

Megan Steele turns to look at the one person in the jury box.

"Megan Steele, you have been charged with ignoring your friends and letting the Vargas Girl contest run your life and getting a swelled head. Does the jury find Megan Steele guilty or not guilty?"

"Guilty as charged," Helen Mae Vorcheck answers.

The loudspeaker broke into my thoughts. The girl from Las Vegas, Nevada, was called first. I felt sorry for her. I'd hate to have been number one. When she returned she headed straight for the rest room with her hand over her mouth. I knew exactly how she felt.

When Carla heard her number called, she turned pale. "Wish me luck," she said. But she didn't wait for my encouragement.

When she returned, her face looked flushed,

and her eyes sparkled. "I think I did great," she said. "I felt really good out there."

Then before I knew it, I heard my number. It never seemed to get any easier to step out onto a stage. *Please let me get through this without doing something dumb.* The blood thundered in my ears, and I could hardly hear Miss Vicky announce my name, age, hometown, and sponsor.

The cameras and the huge crowd made it scarier than ever. I could see the judges in the front row, but I couldn't make out anyone in the audience. I didn't even know if Mom and the Gerritsons had made it in time.

"All right, Megan," Miss Vicky went on. "I want you to look at the teleprompter. On it are the words I want you to say. Keep going, no matter how fast or slowly it moves."

I had no problem with that. Mrs. G made Carla and me read pages of script, over and over until we could do it at any speed. I was surprised she hadn't made us do it standing on our heads.

Miss Vicky asked me to do some of the same things I'd done in the first two contests. This time, I got through them with no disasters.

The stage had been set up like a bedroom. Miss Vicky told me to sit at the dressing table, remove my makeup, then reapply it. "You'll find everything there you'll need. While you do that, I want you to give your prepared speech."

So far, so good. Mrs. G had taught me how to remove makeup correctly. While I applied face cream, I turned to face the judges, and began to talk.

"I imagine you all noticed the hot, dry wind today. Southern California has an unusual weather phenomenon. It's called a Santa Ana, or 'devil's wind.' Winds up to 100 miles per hour come from the east, hurtling through canyons and mountains, and passes toward the sea. Trees get uprooted. Trailers and campers overturn. Small brushfires are whipped into terrifying fire storms.

"The Santa Ana winds also affect people. They could even affect this contest." I paused and pulled out a tissue from a crystal box and began to remove the cream.

"People become irritable and depressed. A famous mystery writer named Raymond Chandler wrote about the desert winds. 'Meek little wives feel the edge of the carving knife and study their husband's necks.'"

I heard the audience laugh and felt encouraged. As I started to apply the makeup base, the bottle slipped out of my greasy fingers and fell to the floor.

I leaned over to reach for it, and felt my zipper give way. Before I could stand up, my dress came apart at the waist. As I grabbed it together, there wasn't a sound from out front. I sat there, bent over and paralyzed, too embarrassed to open my mouth.

Eleven

AS I stood up, still clutching my dress together, I saw Andy and Helen Mae in the second row. They had come to see me, after all. They'd come to see me even though I'd been too busy to spend much time with them. Until that moment, I hadn't realized how much I'd missed both of them.

Although I was sure I'd ruined any chance I had of winning, I kept on giving my speech. "The Santa Anas occur when high pressure air rushes from an upper elevation to a lower one. The air is compressed, and it becomes heated and dry. . . ."

While I talked and started applying new makeup, another part of my mind wondered how the zipper had broken. I'd only worn the dress once. And why had it been so tight?

When I'd bent over, I'd noticed a smirk on Spud's face, and for some reason, my mind jumped to Larry's words, *Hey, Spud, I thought by now your hair would be a lot darker.*

Spud had been in the drugstore. Maybe it wasn't Helen Mae. Maybe Carla put Spud up to switching the bottles in the Sunglow box. And Carla certainly had the opportunity to mess up my dress when she was fixing her dress in my room.

Angry now, I stopped my speech and stopped putting on makeup. Still clutching my dress together, I walked out to the apron of the stage and sat down.

There wasn't a sound in the place. "I'm sorry, Miss Vicky," I said. "I can't finish my prepared speech. There's something more important I have to say."

I could see the audience now, and I looked directly at Andy and Helen Mae. "I have to apologize to two people. They've been my friends practically forever. But ever since I entered this contest, I've been too busy for them. I've been too wrapped up in trying to become the Vargas Girl.

"I really wanted to win the contest, mostly to prove to myself that I could do something besides trip over my own feet. Well, this last disaster with my dress proves that I'll probably always be a klutz. But that doesn't matter anymore.

"You guys are more important to me than winning a contest. I guess I forgot what friendship really means, and I'm sorry—really sorry if I hurt either one of you." A lump in my throat choked me, and I couldn't go on for a second. "Please forgive me."

I stood up again and almost lost my grip on the dress. Nobody in the audience so much as tittered. I walked back to the dressing table to pick up the bottle I'd dropped.

I headed for the dressing room. As soon as Kate saw me, she hurried over. "Megan! What happened to you?"

"Just one of my usual, everyday disasters," I said, trying to make light of it. "My zipper broke, and I nearly lost my dress."

Carla and some of the other girls gathered around me, saying things like, "Oh, I'd just die if that happened to me." And, "I'd be bawling now."

Carla looked so concerned that I wondered if I was wrong about her. "Megan, you must feel awful," she said. "You were gone so long I was getting worried."

"I decided to give a different speech. You were right, Carla. Who wants to hear about the effect the Santa Anas have on people?"

"Turn around and let me look at your dress," Kate said. "You have to go back out onstage pretty soon."

"I'm not going out there again."

I grabbed my jeans and shirt and rushed out to the rest rooms.

Inside a stall, I changed into my old clothes. Then I looked the dress over. The zipper was pulled apart, but it didn't seem to be damaged anywhere. Then I noticed an extra seam sewn into each side—the thread was white, not blue like the original seam. I hadn't gained weight. Carla must have taken the seams in and made the dress too tight. *She must have wanted to be the Vargas Girl awfully badly,* I thought.

Kate came to see if I was all right. "Megan, it's nearly time for the announcement of the five semi-finalists. It's important to me that you finish the contest. I'm your sponsor."

I came out of the stall.

"I don't know what difference it will make," I said. "I've lost any chance I might have had."

Kate gave me an encouraging smile. "What's that sports thing they say—'It's not over till it's over!'"

"It's over for me," I said. Kate hadn't seen how badly I'd botched everything. But if it was important to Kate, then I'd have to see the contest through. I owed her that much. "Okay, I'll go back out onstage."

"Good for you. In this business, you never give up on anything you really want."

But did I really want to be the Vargas Girl anymore? I wasn't so sure.

As we came out of the rest room, we met Carla. "Are you all right, Megan? Is there anything I can do?"

You've done enough for one day, I thought. "I'm fine," I said, and forced a smile. "I guess it's up to you now. I—"

The loudspeaker broke in. "Will the contestants please return to the stage. Come out in single file, according to your number."

"Good luck—both of you," Kate said as Carla and I got into line.

For me to be a semi-finalist, I'd need more than luck. I'd need a miracle.

Out on the stage, I felt really stupid in my old clothes, standing there with the other girls in their beautiful dresses. But I tried to hold my head high.

Miss Vicky gave a little speech so the losers wouldn't feel too bad. "The five finalists tonight will each make a commercial. The girl who makes the best one will go on to the finals in New York. The winner of that contest will be our Vargas Girl. She will receive a thousand dollars, a trip to Hawaii, and will do a series of commercials for the Vargas Schools."

She paused while someone handed her a slip of paper. "This time I'm going to read off the names of the five girls who had the most points, but not in any special order. Please hold your applause until I've announced all five finalists. Kyra Benson, Melody Anderson, Carla Townsend, Stacy Barnes, and Megan Steele."

The audience erupted into applause.

"Take a bow, girls," Miss Vicky said. "Then come on down to the auditorium and join your families and friends for some refreshments."

All the losers gathered around the five of us. A couple were crying, one looked angry, but the rest congratulated us. I'm sure none of them could figure out how I had managed to become a finalist—any more than I could. They probably thought I was Miss Vicky's granddaughter or something.

Carla came over to me. "Isn't it great?" she gushed. "I can't believe *both* of us made it this far."

I'd bet on that, I thought. She must be seething inside, but she did a good job of pretending she was happy that I was a finalist too. "We wouldn't have gotten this far without Mrs. G and Kate's help," was all I said.

Kate came up onto the stage with our stuff, and we went down to join the others.

Mom and Trish nearly strangled me with bear hugs. Mrs. G looked as if she were going to cry.

"I'm not surprised you both won," Scott said. "Mom really knows her stuff in this business."

Both Andy and Helen Mae were standing to one side. A little hesitantly, I went over to them. For a long moment we all just stood there staring. Then Helen Mae and I started toward each other at the same time. We hugged. And I blinked back tears. Andy kept shaking his head. "You're really something—you know that?"

"I—uh—I really meant what I said up there."

Someone handed me a piece of chocolate cake on a fancy paper plate and a cup of fruit punch.

"Watch out, everybody," Spud said, loud enough for people to turn their heads toward us. "The klutz has punch in her hand!"

I was tempted to pretend to trip and spill red punch all over Spud. But I decided not to, because I realized right then that he and Carla couldn't hurt me anymore. Never again would I let them make me feel bad—no matter what mean things they did or said.

It was a wonderful feeling.

Twelve

DURING the week before Carla and I had to make the contest commercial, I had a hard time not saying anything to Carla or Spud. I really wanted to do something mean to both of them.

Yesterday, Carla Townsend and Spud Walters of San Angelo, California, had their most embarrassing moment—in front of hundreds of people. It happened at the $1000-a-plate dinner to raise funds for the election campaign of Ms. Townsend's father. He is the mayor of San Angelo and is running for Congress.

Carla and Spud had just climbed up on the stage to make a few remarks about the mayor. Suddenly, much to the delight of the people who had paid $1000, Carla's and Spud's clothes began to dissolve. . . .

But I managed to keep my mouth shut. I had to do some of my best acting to seem friendly. I was afraid that if Carla suspected I knew what she'd done to my dress, she might do something even worse.

Although Mrs. G worked with Carla and me, I still spent lots of time with Andy and Helen Mae. The Santa Anas were over and the weather was perfect. We went ice-skating and swam in Chris's pool.

Andy took me to see a horror movie. He bought a large box of popcorn, and during a scary scene, I jumped and knocked the box out of his hand. Popcorn flew everywhere. When a piece landed on the head of the man in front of us, Andy and I both got the giggles. People all around kept shushing us.

On the way home, we hardly talked. But it was a nice silence. At my door, Andy took my hands and just looked at me for a minute. "Welcome home, Megan Steele. It's great to have the 'real' Megan back."

* * * * *

On Saturday night before I had to make the commercial, I asked Helen Mae to sleep over.

I'd really missed being around her. We talked and laughed until after midnight, but not once did we mention show business. When I finally drifted off, I had the best night's sleep I'd had since I entered the contest.

I still wanted to do the very best I could. I really did want to be the Vargas Girl and make everybody proud of me—myself most of all. But I wasn't going to let the contest rule my life anymore. I didn't really want to be like Scott who couldn't think of anything except show business.

On Saturday, Mrs. G took Carla and me into Hollywood. She crammed us with last minute information.

"Now, remember, don't change any lines," she told us. "Every single word is important in a commercial. Never touch the mike. Watch out for the 'California lazy tongue'—*fer* instead of for—*warsh* instead of wash—*tuh* instead of *to*."

"We know, we know," Carla said. "We've gone over this stuff a zillion times."

Mrs. G grinned. "I think I'm more nervous than you two are."

"Who's nervous—me nervous?" I said, pretending to bite off all my fingernails. Actually, I felt pretty relaxed. The pressure seemed to be off.

We arrived at a big barn of a studio a good hour ahead of time. "Never be late to an audition or callback," Mrs. G had said a hundred times.

Kids in weird costumes or wearing jeans and shirts sat in the waiting room. They all had large photographs of themselves. "Should we have brought pictures?" I whispered to Mrs. G.

"Not today. But now that you're signed up with Kate, you'll have to have some made."

"Where are Scott and Kate?" Carla asked. "Scott's making the commercial with us, isn't he?"

"Don't worry. He'll be here."

The boy sitting next to me was filling out a sign-in sheet with his name, phone, and clothes size. "Don't we have to do that?" I asked Mrs. G.

"No," she answered. "Miss Vicky has had all your measurements. All five of you contestants will be given a costume to wear in the commercial."

About 20 minutes before our call, the other three semi-finalists and their sponsors came in.

"Hi," Kyra said. "Are you guys nervous?"

"Not me," Carla said smugly. "I never get nervous."

"Lucky you," Kyra told her.

Of all the girls we'd met during the contest, I liked her the most. And I thought she had the best chance of becoming the Vargas Girl.

"When this is all over, let's write to each

other," I said to Kyra.

"Sure. Maybe we can meet sometime. Riverside isn't far from San Angelo."

Suddenly, I heard my name called. I had to go first this time. This was once when I wished I were last.

"Scott, aren't you coming with me?"

He squeezed my hand. "You'll do one segment by yourself. Then you have to change into a costume, and I'll join you."

I took a deep breath and blew it out slowly. "I thought you'd be in there, too."

"Just relax and be yourself. You'll do just fine."

When I walked into the big room and saw the camera and lights and Miss Vicky, all the nervousness came back.

In the first segment, I wore the same clothes I had on—jeans and a T-shirt.

I read the lines just fine, but when I had to sit at a dressing table and put on makeup, disaster struck. I'd never put on false eyelashes before. I got one on crooked. When I glanced in the mirror, I looked as if I were winking all the time. I managed to get them on straight, then knocked over a box of powder and got a sneezing fit.

I thought the director would want me to start over, but the cameraman kept filming away. Everybody else was watching the monitor.

Still coughing a bit from the powder, I sprayed my hair—only I had the opening turned the wrong way and it sprayed all over the mirror.

By now I was so upset that I couldn't even think what to do next. Then I remembered I was supposed to put on lipstick. Bending way down, so I could see in the part of the mirror not covered with hair spray, I grabbed the tube of lipstick. Somehow, I guess because of the weird position, I cracked my elbow on the table. The lipstick made a red streak across my face.

I scrubbed off the mirror with a tissue and stared at myself. I looked like a clown—only nobody was laughing. Ignoring my lines on the big board, I said disgustedly, "Megan the Klutz, you're hopeless."

I put my head down on my arms and began to cry.

Thirteen

MISS Vicky came over to me. I couldn't tell by her expression whether she was angry with me or what. In a very businesslike voice, she told me to change into my costume for the next segment. "One of the teachers from the Hollywood branch of my schools will help you with your hair and makeup."

The segment with Scott went much better. I actually enjoyed making the commercial. When we finished, he gave me a hug. "That was great, Megan. Mom's going to be proud of you."

After I changed and joined the others in the waiting room, everybody wanted to know how I'd done.

"The second part with Scott went okay, but the first part was awful—as usual."

I wanted to be by myself for a while, so I took a walk. I tried to tell myself it didn't matter that I'd ruined the commercial. But it did. I still had something to prove to myself.

When I returned, Carla had just finished her filming. Scott came out with her. "This girl is great. I predict she'll be a star someday."

If it takes stepping on people to make it big—she'll be a superstar. But when she gets to the top, will she have any friends besides Spud? I wondered.

* * * * *

On Sunday Andy invited me out to eat.

"You know what happens to me in restaurants," I said.

"Who said anything about a restaurant? Bring your bathing suit, some sunscreen, and an appetite. I'll pick you up at noon."

When I told my mother, she said, "Good. You need a break after yesterday. But be home early. You have a lot of work to do on Monday. You have orders for three necklaces and two bracelets."

"Andy might want to go to a show or something."

"All right, but be home by eleven. Sharp."

"I will, I promise."

I figured all of the kids would go, but instead, Andy showed up on his bike with a picnic basket strapped onto the back. I got out my bike and backpack, and we took off to the river.

He found a spot by the water where we could watch the ducks. He wouldn't let me do a thing. First, he spread out a blanket. Then he started taking out food. "Mom made the potato salad, the fried chicken came from a take-out place, and the baked beans came from a can, but I made the sandwiches and washed the grapes."

Everything tasted wonderful, and I made a pig of myself. I did save a few crusts to feed the ducks, but the ants were only going to get crumbs.

"Leave room for dessert," he said. "Mr. Yokomura made it especially for you."

When we finished, Andy took a pizza out of the basket. "A pizza?" I said, making a face. "For dessert? It sounds disgusting—sorry, Mr. Yokomura."

"Take a look at it," Andy said.

It looked like a small pizza, but the crust was filled with chocolate cream and pecans and some things I didn't recognize. Andy cut me a slice and put it on a paper plate. "Taste it."

I took a bite, and it melted in my mouth. "This is wonderful. I've never tasted anything so good."

"Now, look at this," Andy said, and handed me a menu from the Pizza Palace. Look under desserts."

I ran my finger down to the desserts, and burst out laughing. The very first item said: *Introducing THE MEGAN, a scrumptious, delectable dessert pizza.*

"This is great! I'm famous now. I have a pizza named after me! Mr. Yokomura's wonderful. I'm going to make him something special." I looked at Andy's beaming face. "But I'll bet it was your idea."

"Well, I might have encouraged him a little."

We packed up the remaining food and spent the day swimming, canoeing, and just talking.

"Megan, I want to apologize for acting like a jerk about Scott. I guess I was jealous of all the time you spent with him."

"He was just trying to help Carla and me. But I was kind of glad you were jealous," I said, avoiding his eyes.

"If you win the contest, you'll be with him even more."

"I don't think you have to worry about that," I said. "There's no way I can win."

I hadn't intended to even talk about the contest any more. As far as I was concerned, it was over.

At dusk we listened to a concert in the park.

I'd never cared much for classical music. But sitting there with Andy, watching the full moon rise, I thought it sounded beautiful.

After the concert, we took a walk along the river and totally lost track of time.

"Oh, my gosh, I'm supposed to be home by eleven." I tried to read my watch by the moonlight. "I think it's after ten-thirty now."

It took us quite a while to walk back to our bikes. By the time we got to my house it was well after eleven. All the lights were out except the back porch light and the night-light in the shop.

At the back door, I whispered, "Thanks for a wonderful, super time. I think it was the best day I've ever had."

"Me, too," he whispered back. "I hope you don't get into trouble. I'll call your mom in the morning and tell her it was all my fault."

I nodded and quietly unlocked the door and slipped inside. I wasn't exactly trying to sneak in, but I'd rather get my lecture in the morning and not spoil the end of a perfect day.

I knew there wasn't much chance of making it to my room, though. My mother never goes to sleep until Trish gets in. But tonight I was in luck. I got past Mom's door without her calling out.

Enough moonlight was shining through my

window so that I could see without turning on a light. Very quietly, I got undressed. Grandma's antique bed always squeaked, so I climbed in carefully. I'd actually made it. I sank back on my pillow, when suddenly the wooden slat that held the springs and mattress gave way. With a crash loud enough to wake the entire neighborhood, mattress, springs, and I landed on the floor.

"Megan Steele! Is that you?"

* * * * *

For my punishment for coming home late, I had to do both my work and Trish's, too, for the next two weeks. Plus, I had to clean my room from top to bottom. Helen Mae came over and helped me with that. There are so many kids in her family that she's good at organizing drawers and closets.

Between my work in the shop and the extra chores, I hardly had time to think about the contest.

We received an invitation, printed in silver script on gray paper, inviting me and my family and any special friends to Victoria Vargas's house in Beverly Hills. It was a party to announce the name of the contestant who would go to the finals in New York.

Trish and I listened on the extension while Mom called Kate to find out what we should wear. "Formal," Kate said. "Very formal."

"But my dress is ruined," I put in.

"Don't worry about it," Kate said. "You'll wear the same outfit you wore in the commercial. You'll change at Miss Vicky's mansion."

"I won't have to do anything, will I?" I asked.

"I doubt it. I know they're going to show the commercials that each of you made."

"Oh, no! Even the awful one?"

Kate laughed. "Nearly everybody wants to climb in a hole and hide when they see themselves on TV for the first time."

I planned to dig a hole all the way to China.

Mom and Kate talked for a few minutes more about how to find the mansion. "You can't miss it," Kate said. "It's enormous, and looks like a castle."

Trish poked me and whispered, "Try not to fall in the moat!"

We only invited Helen Mae and Chris, Larry, and a few friends of Mom's. Naturally the Gerritsons had received an invitation. Carla's parents invited almost everybody in city hall, newspaper reporters, and half the business people in town it seemed like.

*　*　*　*　*

When we pulled up in front of the huge, gray stone mansion, uniformed attendants helped us out and parked the car.

As we went inside, I felt as if I'd stepped into a movie set. I thought Chris's house was big, but this place made his look like a summer cabin.

Mom told the butler that I was one of the contestants, and he took me right to Miss Vicky.

She looked beautiful in her usual gray and silver. For once she wasn't wearing a hat. "Welcome, my dear," she said, and gave me a peck on the cheek. "You're the last candidate to arrive."

Smiling and nodding to everyone, we made our way through the crowd to a room where the other girls were changing.

"As soon as you girls are ready, come to the ballroom and take seats in the first row. And don't look so scared. The hard part is over."

I nodded to Carla, who was busily combing her hair. Nobody said much as we got ready. I slipped into my costume, a white and silver ballgown that fit me perfectly. All the dresses were white and silver, but each was a slightly different style.

"Carla? How about zipping me up?" I

asked, looking her straight in the eyes.

"I—oh, I have lipstick on my fingers," she said quickly. "Ask Kyra."

"Sure," I said. "I wouldn't want anything to happen to this dress." I was proud of myself. I wanted her to stew a bit and worry about whether I knew what she'd done.

When we were all ready, we headed for the ballroom and took our seats. As big as the room was, it was packed. Mom and the Gerritsons and my friends were sitting near the front. They were all so happy now. In a few minutes, they'd want to disown me.

A servant blinked the light twice to warn people that the presentation was about to begin.

Miss Vicky came forward and stood on a raised platform in front of a huge screen. "I'd like to welcome all the families and friends of our five semi-finalists. Some of you have come from as far as Nevada and Washington. I know you're all as proud of these girls as I am. To have reached this far in the Vargas Girl contest is quite an achievement. I'm just sorry only one of them will go on to the finals in New York next week.

"First we're going to show you the commercials the girls made. Even though four of them won't win tonight, I'm sure they all have a future in show business, if that's their desire. We have chosen the order of the commercials by lot. After we watch all five, there will be a 30-minute intermission. Please help yourself to the refreshments."

Melody Anderson's commercials were shown first. I thought she seemed a little stiff, but she looked really pretty. Kyra Benson came next. I still thought she had the best chance of winning—until I watched Carla. Scott was right. She probably would be a star someday. As much as I hated to admit it, she was great. You'd have thought she'd been making commercials for years.

Next, they showed mine. When I saw myself on the screen, I wanted to crawl under the chair. As I watched myself spilling powder and spraying the mirror, I wanted to disappear from the face of the earth. People started snickering, then everybody was laughing. I slid further and further down in my chair and closed my eyes. I couldn't bear to watch any more.

I just sat there, my mind blank, my eyes closed, waiting for intermission so I could leave.

But when the lights came on, Mom and Trish and my friends rushed over to me. Everybody said I did just fine in the second part. No one even mentioned the awful first segment. I knew they were all trying to make me feel better.

"It's okay," I said. "I knew last week that I'd blown any chance I had of winning. It's no big deal."

"Megan?"

I turned to see Joe and Gloria from the TV station. "We just wanted to tell you that we're taping all the parts with you and Carla," Gloria said. "You know, like a local-girls-make-good story."

I wanted to say "Please burn my part," but Gloria said, "Be sure to watch next Saturday—unless you're on your way to New York, of course. In any case, we'll see that you get a copy."

She looked around. "Have you seen Carla? I want to tell her, too."

"I saw her talking to Spud Walters," Andy said. "Over by the food." Joe and Gloria headed for the refreshment tables.

"Let's go get some punch," Andy said to me. And before I could answer, he pulled me off to one side. "I know how you must feel, Megan. But honestly, it wasn't bad at all. When you're klutzy, you're cute and funny."

"Thanks, Andy. It's okay. You don't need to try to cheer me up. At least Carla was good. All the work your mom did to help us didn't go to waste."

"Look at Carla now," he said, and nodded toward the tables of food.

Her father had his arm around Carla, and in the voice he uses for campaign speeches, he said, "Am I crazy or is my little girl going to be the Vargas Girl?" Their crowd of friends all clapped.

Someone asked her if she was all packed to go to New York. Carla laughed. "I'm already packed for the trip to Hawaii. You should see my new bikini."

"Let's get out of here for a few minutes," Andy said. "I don't want to listen to her."

"Carla's probably not as confident as she sounds. But I would like to get out of this noisy crowd for a while."

We managed to find our way to a door that led to a garden. The balmy air carried the scent of roses and star jasmine. We talked for a bit. Then I said, "I suppose we should go back inside."

When we got to the ballroom, Miss Vicky was already at the table in front of the mike. "In a few minutes we will show the speeches given at the semi-finals. But I have just been given some very distressing news about one of the contestants."

Fourteen

ANDY and I looked at each other. "I wonder what that's all about," I whispered.

"Maybe one of the contestants is sick or something," Andy said.

Miss Vicky looked really upset. She absently picked at the flower in a silver bowl on the table. "There will be a slight delay. Please return to the refreshment tables and make yourselves at home until you see the lights dim. And now, I'd like the five contestants and their sponsors to come to my study."

Andy squeezed my hand. "I hope it's nothing too serious."

As the other girls and I followed Miss Vicky, they all looked as bewildered as I felt.

The study was enormous. Our town library isn't much bigger.

"Please sit down everybody," Miss Vicky said quietly.

When we'd all found chairs, she went on. "I hardly know where to begin. I just cannot believe something like this has happened."

She took a deep breath as though she hated to even talk about it. "During intermission, I learned that one of the semi-finalists did something unethical. She deliberately tried to hurt the chances of another contestant." Miss Vicky avoided looking directly at any of us. "I won't make this public, but obviously the girl will no longer be a part of this contest nor associated in any way with the Vargas schools."

Melody's sponsor spoke up. "But that isn't fair. Anybody could come to you with a madeup story."

"My sources had no reason to lie. On the contrary, I think it must have been a difficult decision for them to come to me."

Out of the corners of my eyes, I tried to see if any of the girls looked guilty, but I couldn't tell by their expressions. They all looked stunned.

"That's all I have to say—except that I'm very disappointed. Now, you may return to your seats. We will continue with the presentations."

Nobody said a word as we went back to the ballroom. Carla sat next to me. "I'll bet it was

Melody Anderson," Carla whispered. "But I wonder what she did?"

I just shrugged and stared straight ahead. *Could someone know about what Carla did to me?* I hardly heard Miss Vicky announce the next presentation. "After the speeches, I will give you the judges' decision. We stayed up half the night reviewing the tapes of the first contests. But I'm happy to say our decision was unanimous."

The lights dimmed, and Kyra Benson's face showed up on the big screen. She talked about hunger in Africa. The first three girls talked about serious subjects. They all got a big hand from the audience.

Carla was next. She looked really good as she put on makeup and talked about her dream of being a famous model. "All my life I've known what I wanted to do. I used to dress up in my mother's clothes and high heels and pretend I was a fashion model."

She talked some more, then looked right toward the camera. "But my biggest dream is to be someone just like Victoria Vargas."

I groaned. *Oh, Carla,* I thought, *don't be so obvious.* But she got more applause than anyone else had.

Then my face showed up on the screen. I saw myself putting on cold cream, and heard myself start my prepared speech about the Santa Anas. Then I dropped the bottle, leaned over, and my dress came apart.

It seemed so strange to watch myself sit on the edge of the stage and apologize to Helen Mae and Andy.

"I really wanted to win the contest, mostly to prove to myself that I could do something besides trip over my own feet. Well, this last disaster with my dress proves that I'll probably always be a klutz. But that doesn't matter anymore. . . ."

When the film showed me hesitate, I got a lump in my throat just as I had onstage, and I blinked back tears. "Please forgive me."

As the screen went dark, I heard people clearing their throats. Then the lights came up, and Miss Vicky came back to the mike.

"Aren't you proud of these girls? Let's give them a big hand."

When the applause died down, she went on. "As you saw from the commercials, all the girls did very well. But what we are really looking for is someone with whom the average young girl can identify."

I only half listened to Miss Vicky. I was thinking about Carla.

"She needs to be naturally pretty, someone you'd like to know," Miss Vicky said.

Carla nudged me. She smoothed her hair and licked her lips to make them glisten. "Do I look all right?" she whispered. "I'd like to put on some lipstick, but the TV people are filming us."

I glanced over to the aisle. I hadn't even noticed Gloria and Joe with their camera. "You look great," I whispered back to Carla. She was amazing. She was so sure she'd won. I wished I had as much confidence as she did.

"You did really well," she said generously. "Especially considering all the things that went wrong."

"Ladies and gentlemen," Miss Vicky was saying, "may I present the judges' unanimous decision—" She paused for effect.

Carla turned and gave her father a triumphant smile.

"Megan Steele," Miss Vicky finished.

As the crowd applauded wildly, Carla's face turned scarlet. She sank down in her chair as if all the wind had been knocked out of her.

I looked at the other girls. "There must be a mistake," I said. "You were all much better—"

Kyra jumped up and hugged me. "No. You deserve to win. Good luck in New York."

Then everybody was hugging me, and the TV camera was practically in my face.

Carla grabbed my arm and pulled me to

one side. Her face was all mottled gray and red. "You rotten snitch," she hissed at me. "I'd have won if you hadn't told Miss Vicky about your hair and your dress!"

I looked around at the people watching us. "Carla," I whispered, "I never said a word to anybody."

"You're a liar! You—"

Gloria broke in. "It wasn't Megan," she said quietly. "Joe and I overheard you talking to your friend. You were gloating about how you'd sunk Megan. Anyway, the judges picked her last night—long before I told Miss Vicky about you."

Carla started to bluster, then tears welled to her eyes. "My dad's never going to forgive me."

I couldn't help feeling a little sorry for her. "Carla, winning this contest isn't that important. Everybody says you have a great future in show business."

Carla avoided my eyes. "I'll pay to have your dress fixed. Good luck in New York," she mumbled. I knew that was as close to an apology as I'd ever get.

I never have been able to stay mad at Carla. We've known each other too long. Before I could say any more, Miss Vicky clapped her hands for attention. "Now, that you've all had a chance to congratulate our winner, I want to offer my own congratulations. Megan, my dear, will you come up here, please?"

I hurried over to the table. She kissed me on both cheeks. "I'm extremely proud of you, Megan. You were able to overcome obstacles with dignity, warmth, and humor. But I must say it's with some misgiving that I ask you to join me here." She smiled broadly, and looked out at the audience. "You see, in her first contest, she managed to get me soaking wet."

My face got hot. "I'm really sorry about that," I said quickly.

"Frankly, it was all your mishaps that were responsible for your win. As you said in an interview with Gloria Carruthers, 'If a klutzy person can win a contest, *anyone* can.' Well, that's what our commercials will say. If a klutzy person can come to a Victoria Vargas School of Modeling and Self-improvement and learn to be poised and self-assured during any calamity, then *anybody* can.

"If I didn't know better, I'd think Megan had been attending one of my schools all her life. Congratulations again, my dear."

In a daze I heard the laughter and applause. Then suddenly my family and friends were all around me.

"Watch out, New York," Andy said. "Here comes Megan."

As I looked around at my friends, I no longer cared what happened in New York. As I'd said to Carla—winning wasn't all that important. I didn't need to be the Vargas Girl. I'd already proven to myself that I could do something without tripping over my own feet.

But then I went to hug my mom, and I tripped over the microphone cord. The mike tipped over, hit Miss Vicky a glancing blow on the arm, and knocked into the table. Water from a bowl of flowers splashed all over Miss Vicky's gown.

Oh, no! Not again! I just closed my eyes and whispered, "Megan the Klutz strikes again!"

About the Author

ALIDA E. YOUNG lives with her husband in the high desert of southern California. When she's not researching or writing a new novel, she enjoys taking long walks. To help her write her novels, she likes to put herself in her characters' shoes, to try to feel things the way they would.

Alida says, "I'm the original klutz. Once, I sprayed my husband's shirt with window cleaner instead of spray starch. Another time, instead of using hair spray, I spritzed my hair with deodorant. I used to perform in plays, and many of the things that happen to poor Megan, happened to me."

Alida's books have made her an award-winning author. In 1990 her novel *Too Young To Die* was named a winner in the national Book-It competition.

Other books by Alida include *Is My Sister Dying?*, *Dead Wrong*, and *Earthquake!* She has also written adventure novels, including *Terror in the Tomb of Death* and *Return to the Tomb of Death*.

Be sure to look for *Megan the Klutz*, Alida's first book in this popular series.